Nothing much seemed to surprise Marc Hammond.

Not much surprised Robin either; she was used to the unexpected happening around her. Half the time she didn't know why it happened, and most of the time she didn't know how to deal with it.

Marc had said that *she* was a time bomb, but of all the men Robin had ever met Marc Hammond was the one who seemed to pack so much dynamic energy that she couldn't imagine life would ever be calm around him.

Jane Donnelly began earning her living as a writer as a teenage reporter. When she married the editor of the newspaper she freelanced for women's mags for a while, and wrote her first Mills & Boon romance as a hard-up single parent. Now she lives in a roses-round-the-door cottage near Stratford upon Avon, with her daughter, four dogs and assorted rescued animals. Besides writing she enjoys travelling, swimming, walking and the company of friends.

LIVING WITH MARC

BY
JANE DONNELLY

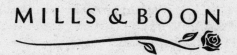

MILLS & BOON

First published in Great Britain 1996
Harlequin Mills & Boon Limited,
Eton House, 18–24 Paradise Road, Richmond, Surrey TW9 1SR

© Jane Donnelly 1996

ISBN 0 263 79942 5

Set in 10 on 12 pt Linotron Times
02-9701-54224-D

Typeset in Great Britain by CentraCet, Cambridge
Printed and bound in Great Britain
by Mackays of Chatham PLC, Chatham

CHAPTER ONE

ROBIN had thought the day could not get worse, but when she saw who was sitting behind that desk she had to bite her lip hard or she would have shrieked with hysterical laughter. The sight of Robin was a shock to him too. It took a lot to shake Marc Hammond, but one of the heavy dark eyebrows raised a fraction as he gasped, 'Good Lord!'

'Good afternoon and goodbye,' Robin gulped.

She was turning to leave when he asked, 'Whatever made you imagine you'd be suitable for the job?'

Robin hadn't exchanged a word with Marc Hammond for years. But the way he was putting her down now—a big man behind a big desk, so sure of himself in every way—brought back memories.

Last time she had seen him she'd been seventeen and tongue-tied. Now, a few years older, and after one heck of a morning, her self-control cracked. Rage flared in her, bright as her tumbling red hair, and she was across the room, gripping the edge of the desk, leaning over and facing him.

'Because,' she snapped, 'the advert was for a companion-driver to an elderly lady and I reckon I'd be efficient on both counts, but I know you wouldn't employ me any way, any time, so we have both wasted a few minutes.'

He was leaning back in his chair, chin in hand, watching her as if she was making a show of herself.

'The old lady in question,' he drawled drily, 'has had

more than enough excitement over the years. What she's needing now is peace and quiet, and I don't suppose there's much of that around you.'

She should not have flared up. She should have stayed cool-headed. She made a belated attempt to retrieve a little dignity, straightening up, letting her hands fall to her sides, saying, 'Sorry,' although she had nothing to apologise to him for. 'It's been one of those days.'

'Have a lot of them, do you?' he enquired.

More than you, she thought. I bet not much goes wrong with your day, or your life. She shrugged. 'Not too many. But no job, of course.'

'No job.'

If he was doing the interviewing the old lady had to be somebody close to him. He'd never consider Robin, and she couldn't have taken on work that might have kept her under Marc Hammond's eye.

When he got up she remembered how tall he was. She was over average height herself, but as he came round the desk he was towering over her and she found herself backing towards the door. 'I'll see you out,' he said.

'No need. I know the way.' The front door had been opened by a woman who looked like a housekeeper. The office where Marc Hammond had been waiting led off the hall, and Robin did not want him walking anywhere beside her. But he ignored her protests; he was seeing her out, and she bit back the urge to say, You don't have to watch that I'm leaving empty-handed; I won't pocket any of the silver.

The wide floor of the hall was of polished wood, there were rugs in dark jewel colours and the paintings all looked like pricey originals.

When Robin had turned from the road into a curving drive leading to a house with white pillars and three storeys of long white windows, she had thought, Wow!

The advertisement had had a phone number and she had been given this address. She hadn't known who lived here but she had hoped it was the elderly lady who was advertising, because it had looked such a super place to work in. That, of course, was before she had known Marc Hammond was here. Now she couldn't get out of the house fast enough.

He said nothing to her as they walked down the hall. He might have managed a goodbye when he'd opened the door, but just before they reached it somebody called, 'Robin?' and Robin whirled round as an elderly woman came tripping down the stairs with a wide, welcoming smile. 'Robin? It is Robin?' And the woman she knew as Mrs Myson threw her arms around her. 'What are you doing here?'

'I—I came about the job,' Robin stammered.

'You never. You did?' She clasped her hands together and almost did a little dance. 'But this is marvellous. Marc, how did you find her?'

Marc Hammond looked down on them both. 'I didn't,' he said shortly. 'Where did you?'

'You mean she just came along?' Mrs Myson had silver hair, beautifully styled, and an almost unlined face. Now her blue eyes sparkled as Robin explained.

'I answered the ad in Friday's paper. Are you the lady who needs a driver?' Mrs Myson nodded. 'I didn't know that.'

'And I didn't know you were Miss Johnson.' Neither had Marc Hammond. There were lots of Johnsons around although none of them was related to Robin.

If she had said 'Robin Johnson' instead of just 'Johnson' he would never have interviewed her.

'I didn't know you were looking for a job.' Mrs Myson's smile was mischievous. 'Between you and me, I don't really think there is a job, but now I know you're interested I'm changing my mind.' Her smile took them both in. 'Well, isn't this lovely?'

'I'd put it another way.' Marc Hammond was tight-lipped, unsmiling. 'Where did you two meet?'

'Oh, we're old friends,' the old lady said blithely. That wasn't quite true.

'*Where?*' he persisted.

'At the Sunday market,' Mrs Myson said, and now she was holding both Robin's hands. Getting the job that had been advertised would have been brilliant, because Robin liked Mrs Myson. But with Marc Hammond calling the odds her chances were nil.

The Sunday market was held weekly on the old airfield in countryside a few miles out of town. Anyone could hire a pitch and Robin often turned up to help an old schoolfriend. Amy was a single mother short on funds, who had a flair for sewing and 'did' local jumble sales, bought items cheaply then laundered and mended and sometimes restyled, and offered very wearable clothes at very reasonable prices.

When Robin helped with the selling, trade always improved, because Robin jollied the customers. The market was popular; customers arrived from miles around. When Robin smiled at them most folk smiled back, and in no time she would be helping them find a bargain.

Mrs Myson had been on the charity stall the morning Robin had been buying a little china ballerina, for a friend's birthday, from the bric-a-brac section. 'I used

to have red hair. Not as beautiful as yours, but red,'
the old lady serving had told her. Robin had liked her
on sight. Her gaiety of spirit had made a little bond
between them and Robin had looked out for her in the
months that had followed.

Mrs Myson was usually on the charity stall. She
turned up for all sorts of good causes, from a country
ravaged by war or drought or earthquakes to the local
cats' home. And although she was always cheerful
Robin wondered if she had a lonely life outside her
charity fund-raising.

If the old lady lived in this house and the powerful
Marc Hammond was watching out for her, she was
hardly alone, but Robin felt she would have quite
enjoyed being Maybelle Myson's companion. There
was a refreshing spark of devilment in the old lady,
and when Marc said, '*You* work on a charity stall?' as
if he couldn't believe that Robin would be helping
anybody but herself, Mrs Myson defended her
indignantly.

'Yes, Robin has helped on the stall.' A couple of
times when Robin had found Mrs Myson alone and
busy she had given a hand. 'And last week she helped
us pack up when we had that cloudburst.' Mrs Myson
was still holding Robin's hands. 'You are taking the
job?'

'I've already been turned down.' Robin smiled as
she spoke because it was best to treat this lightly.

'Why?' Mrs Myson was bewildered, looking at Marc
for an explanation.

'The idea is to find you a congenial companion who
can drive a car and keep an eye on you,' he said
wearily. 'I know you think you could still ferry a raft
up the Amazon but you need reminding that you are

eighty-two years old, and I have no intention of letting you loose with a juvenile delinquent.'

'What did you say?' Robin glared; she couldn't help it. 'I am not a juvenile.' Not even a teenager. Twenty years old today, and so far it had been the kind of birthday she wouldn't wish on her worst enemy. 'Nor am I a delinquent,' she snapped. 'I could sue you for saying that.'

'Only if you got yourself a very good lawyer.' That had to be a joke of sorts; Marc Hammond, head of Hammond and Hammond, was the smartest lawyer she was ever likely to meet.

Deadpan, she said, 'Ha, ha.' And Mrs Myson protested.

'That wasn't a very nice thing to say, Marc. What's so unsuitable about Robin? Why shouldn't she be—' she pulled a face as if this was a silly description '—a lady's companion?'

He showed real exasperation for the first time, his voice suddenly harsh, 'For God's sake, look at her.'

Robin knew what he meant by that. Her hair was so bright a red that only those who had known her since she was a child believed that it was natural, and she wore it almost waist-length. But even when it was tucked away under a hat Robin Johnson was still a knockout. She had a model girl's long-legged figure, with high cheekbones, a wide mouth and restless green eyes. Without deliberately doing a thing, Robin was a stirrer. Around her, life quickened and sometimes got out of hand.

She knew how she was looking now—her cheeks flushed and her eyes glinting, because Marc Hammond had that effect on her—but Mrs Myson seemed to see nothing wrong in her appearance. 'I can't believe you'd

turn Robin down just because she's young,' Mrs Myson
said.

Marc Hammond smiled at that. Cynically. And his
voice was sarcastic, as he said, 'I take back the juvenile;
I'm sure Miss Johnson is old for her years.'

'Thanks a lot,' Robin muttered. She managed to get
one hand free from Mrs Myson, who had a very firm
grip for someone in her eighties.

'But you still think she might be too hot to handle?'
Mrs Myson was teasing Marc and he was looking at
her with amused tolerance.

'Something like that,' he said. 'She certainly was last
time.'

'Last time?' the elderly lady echoed.

'When she worked for me,' said Marc Hammond.
'Briefly.'

'Oh, dear.' Mrs Myson was smiling. 'This has to
mean there was some sort of trouble.'

'There would have been,' he said drily, and Robin
flared up.

'Don't make it sound as if I was robbing the till.'

There had been no tills in that office. Hammond and
Hammond were the top law firm in town, the building
they occupied was one of the most impressive, and
Robin had arrived there as a trainee receptionist.

And had met Marc Hammond. She had seen him
crossing the foyer—a tall, dark, strikingly good-looking
man. He had come across, looked hard at her and
welcomed her to the firm. She had gulped, feeling her
breath catch in her throat, and she had still been
holding her breath when he'd walked away. After that
he hadn't seemed to notice her at all until her first
Friday.

Others had. A studious, bespectacled junior clerk

had fancied her from the first day, and when Robin had had lunch with him he had gone back to the office on cloud nine. He'd even grinned at the husky biker in studded leather who had been leaning on the counter under the disapproving eye of the senior receptionist, until the biker had come over and knocked him flat.

The clerk's first impression was that here was a homicidal maniac, and for the first time in his life, and probably the last, he started frantically to fight back.

Robin shrieked. She knew the biker. She had had a very brief fling with him and wanted no more. She yelled, 'Stop it, you idiots,' but the biker went on throwing the punches and, seeing blood, the receptionist gave a high-pitched scream that went on and on.

Hammond and Hammond was a law firm. Folk came into their offices carrying a load of grief and resentment, but there had never been a scene as physically violent as this, a rough and tumble between two men, fists and feet flying, and a girl with long flaming red hair dodging around screaming their names and trying to shove them apart.

When Marc Hammond came down the stairs Robin didn't see him until he yanked the biker away and threw him through the door into the street. Jack was two hundred and ten pounds but he went out bodily, hardly touching the ground.

Then Hammond turned on his employees. 'Right, you two—in my office,' he said.

The receptionist was moaning now, staring at the spots of blood on Robin's white shirt. There was more on the junior clerk because it was his nose which was bleeding, although it didn't show up on his dark suit. He dug into his pocket for a tissue, trying to staunch the flow as they trailed after Marc Hammond, through a small, empty office into a large room with panelled walls and a huge desk with a black leather top.

Hammond closed the door and Robin thought that she and the clerk must look a wretched pair. Tony had realised he had been fighting with Robin's boyfriend in front of Hammond himself and that this was probably going to cost him his job. His nose was sore, and he'd lost his glasses, so that he could hardly see. But he could see enough for Marc Hammond, still immaculate and cool as a cucumber, to look more formidable than a gang of roughnecks.

Robin was flushed and breathing fast, her hair all over the place, and miserably aware that most of this was her fault. The young man blinked, head ducked. Robin looked up at Marc Hammond and wondered if there was any way she could plead for her colleague.

'You'd better clean up and go home for the day,' he said.

'Yessir,' the clerk mumbled into his bloodstained tissue as he stumbled blindly out of the room.

Then Hammond turned his attention to Robin. There was a scorching feeling of danger about him. She could feel the heat burning her cheeks.

'Has this kind of thing happened before?' he was demanding.

She nearly said no. But once or twice it had, so she muttered, 'Well—'

'I thought so. Well, *you* might get a kick out of two men fighting over you but our clients don't expect to walk into a blood bath when they come through the door.'

She was getting the sack. Aunt Helen had been right. 'You'll never keep a job there,' she'd said when Robin had told her and Uncle Edward that she'd had an interview and was starting on Monday. This would be just what Aunt Helen had expected, but all through lunch the young clerk had been talking about *his* career prospects. He was so pleased to be working here.

'What will happen to him?' she asked. 'It wasn't his fault.'

'I can believe that,' Hammond drawled. 'Somebody like Tony wouldn't stand much of a chance if you moved in on him.'

That was not what she'd meant. She hadn't made the moves. The first day she'd arrived he had asked for a date and gone on asking, but it was not until today she'd agreed just to have a sandwich with him. She said, 'I meant the fight; Jack hit him first.'

'I'm sure he did. I think Tony's ego has been damaged enough for one week. We can forget him. The problem is you.' She felt even younger than she was, standing there while he passed judgement on her. 'I've no doubt you'll make your mark,' he said drily. 'But not in my firm. And I hope you don't do too much damage to others on the way.'

She went downstairs to get her coat. The receptionist was dealing with a smartly dressed man and woman and avoided looking Robin's way, and Robin thought that it was just as well they hadn't arrived five minutes earlier. They didn't look the sort to be impressed by a member of the firm having a punch-up with a biker.

Now, three years later, the biker had long gone. Robin might have passed the clerk in town since without noticing him, but they'd certainly never spoken another word to each other.

'So what happened?' Mrs Myson was wanting to know. She looked from Robin to Marc and he answered.

'Three years ago, you were with us how long?' He knew how long, Robin would bet. 'Nearly a week, wasn't it?' She nodded and he told Mrs Myson, 'Two of her admirers had a fight in the foyer.'

'The office foyer?'

'That's the one.'

She crowed with laughter. 'I never heard about it.'

'We kept it quiet.' His grin took the sternness from his face, making him look suddenly light-hearted. 'We didn't want rumours getting around that dissatisfied clients were beating up the staff. The only witness was Edna Hodgkiss, and you know what a soul of discretion she is.'

Mrs Myson wasn't shocked; her eyes were twinkling. But Robin knew the joke was on her. At just seventeen she had wanted to crawl away. Now she would have said, I didn't get a kick out of it. They're a couple of morons, like a lot of the men I seem to meet, and that's their problem, not mine.

Mrs Myson waved the matter away. 'This happened years ago; it's all forgotten by now, and Robin needs a job. You say I need a companion. Well, I'd like Robin.'

'We've had much more suitable applicants, and you've turned them all down,' said Marc Hammond.

'I didn't want them,' said Mrs Myson. She nearly pouted, and Robin glimpsed the dazzling, demanding girl she must have been, and still was under the skin.

'No way,' he said implacably.

Robin pulled her other hand clear but Mrs Myson had her at once by the elbow and was smiling sweetly at Marc. 'At least Robin must stay to tea.'

'No, thank you,' Robin said promptly. She would choke trying to swallow while he watched her.

'With me,' said Maybelle Myson. 'I am allowed

guests, aren't I?' That was another joke, and again he shook his head at her, a smile lifting the edge of a mouth that Robin would have likened to a rat-trap.

'I'll tell Elsie to bring up a tray,' he said.

'This way, my dear,' said Maybelle.

As she followed the old lady up the wide staircase Robin didn't have to look back to know that Marc Hammond was still standing in the hallway below, watching her. She could feel his eyes on her almost like a hand shoving her, so that she took every step carefully as if she might stumble.

She hadn't realised the effect that meeting him again face to face might have on her. She would never forget how she was sacked; it had been so humiliating. But it was more than three years ago. Since then she had had her share of bad scenes and she had thought she was tough.

She was tough. She had had to be. She had learned as a child not to wear her heart on her sleeve or to show hurt or anger unless she was unbearably provoked. But Marc Hammond seemed to storm through her defences. She found herself almost holding her breath, until they reached the top of the stairs and she followed Mrs Myson into a room and the door closed behind them, shutting him out down in the hall.

This was a sitting room. Chairs and a long sofa were covered in pale blue silk. There were fresh flowers— an arrangement of freesias and roses. Their perfume filled the air. It was a delightful room.

Mrs Myson sat with her feet up on the sofa and Robin took a low stool. Mrs Myson began telling her about some of the other applicants for the job. Some of them sounded reasonable to Robin, although Maybelle Myson had been dead set against every one—almost as prejudiced as Marc Hammond was against Robin, and Robin was the one she couldn't have.

'I can't tell you how pleased I am that you turned up,' Maybelle said.

'He won't let me stay,' Robin pointed out.

'We'll see.' Maybelle gave a little nod, and Robin wondered if the old lady would go against Marc Hammond's advice. Perhaps he was here in a professional capacity, as her lawyer, although that was not at all how it had seemed.

'Are you related?' she asked. Maybelle could have been his grandmother.

'Marc's grandmother was my sister,' she said. 'I'm his aunt—well, his great-aunt. We had no children. I would have liked a daughter, a granddaughter.' Briefly she sounded wistful, then her eyes filled with tenderness. 'But Marc has always been like a son to me. Better than most sons I hear about.'

There was a tap on the door and the woman who had let 'Miss Johnson' into the house came into the room carrying a tray. Maybelle Myson thanked her and she put down the tray on a side-table, pausing to give Robin a long, hard stare from head to foot before she went out.

The tray was laid with tiny sandwiches, a Dundee cake, cream, sugar and lemon, and a teapot, cups, saucers and plates in beautiful china.

Robin poured, and took lemon tea because the amber liquid and the lemon rind looked so pretty in the eggshell-thin white cup. She took a bite of cake, letting the crumbs melt on her tongue, listening to Maybelle Myson.

Until now Robin had known next to nothing about

Maybelle. She was always well dressed and anyone could see she was a lady in the true sense of the word— but their talk had always been cheerful chatter—no heart-to-hearts or confidences. But somehow Robin had felt they were on the same wavelength in spite of an age gap of a couple of generations.

Now, as they took tea together, she listened enthralled while Maybelle talked, telling Robin she had been a widow for years. Her husband had been an engineer and they had travelled the world together. Marc Hammond was right; Maybelle Myson had had a life packed with adventure in far-away places.

Listening had Robin on the edge of her chair, because it was nearly like being there herself. One of Robin's dreams was to really travel—not to holiday resorts but somewhere explorers and archaeologists went—and although Marc Hammond could stop her getting a job here he probably wouldn't stop her keeping in touch. Or coming to tea, perhaps. Because the more she saw and learned of Maybelle Myson, the more she liked her.

Several times Mrs Myson had started to ask Robin about herself but Robin had answered briefly and got Maybelle back to her memories. They were fascinating and, to Robin, Robin's own life was not. She would much rather hear how a bridge had been built over a raging river in a jungle than talk about herself. Although, after their second cup of tea and when most of the sandwiches had gone, Maybelle Myson said firmly, 'Now, tell me about yourself.'

'What do you want to know?' Robin asked.

'Well, where do you live?'

'At home. With my aunt and uncle. They've brought

me up since I was five, when my mother died. She was my mother's sister.'

Maybelle Myson said, 'Like Marc's grandmother and me.' She went on gaily, 'I always approve of aunts.'

You would not approve of mine, thought Robin, but she managed to keep her voice light and bright, asking, 'Are you really eighty-two? You don't took anywhere near that.'

She was not trying to flatter. Maybelle Myson could have knocked ten or more years off her age and got away with it easily, and now she said, 'Thank you,' and laughed. 'Most of the time I feel, say, fifty-something, although there are days when I am every minute of my age, but don't tell anyone that.' Robin laughed with her. 'How old are you, Robin?' she enquired.

'Twenty.' Robin thought for a moment before she added, 'Today,' because it had been a grim birthday.

Of course Maybelle said, 'Twenty today? How lovely for you. You must be very happy.' Robin kept on smiling although bitter laughter was churning inside her. 'I was married before I was twenty,' Maybelle reminisced. 'He was so handsome.' She got off the sofa and went to a drawer. Robin expected photographs and leaned forward, but she came back holding something in the palm of her hand.

'Happy birthday,' she said, and into Robin's hand she dropped a heavy chain bracelet. Three chunky charms hung from the fastener-ring: a cross, an anchor and a heart. 'Faith, hope and charity,' said Maybelle. 'With those you can't go far wrong.'

It looked like gold, and a gift had been the last thing that Robin had expected. She felt tears welling in her eyes and blinked them away fiercely. She never shed

tears in front of anyone, but after this morning, and
after Marc Hammond, she was vulnerable to kindness
and this was such a generous gesture.

'That is so kind of you,' she said. 'I do appreciate it
and it is beautiful, but of course I couldn't take it
unless—' She bit her lip. This was awkward. 'Is it gold?
Is it as real as it looks?'

'Yes.'

'Then no, thank you. Please, I'd feel awful taking
something this valuable.'

'Nonsense,' said Maybelle briskly, but when Robin
shook her head and gave the bracelet back she took it,
keeping hold of Robin's wrist. 'Well, try it on.'

There was no harm in that. It was weighty on
Robin's slim wrist. She had never worn anything like
it before and it should surely have been an heirloom.
She said again, 'It's beautiful but I can't take it.'

Maybelle did her mischievous twinkle. 'Wear it
while you're on duty.'

'What? Oh, we can forget that. I'm not going to be
on duty here.' As she spoke she had a pang of regret
because she could have been the right one for this job,
given half a chance. Which she would not be getting
from Marc Hammond.

'Marc is going to make me have a driver,' said
Maybelle. 'And a companion. A minder is what he has
in mind. He'd wrap me in cotton wool if he could and
sometimes that can be comforting.'

Sometimes it must be, thought Robin, who had
never had a protector who did not ask more from her
than he offered. 'So,' said Maybelle Myson, 'we must
bring him round to accepting you.'

'He won't.'

Robin was sure of that. The vibes between them had

been as threatening as a collision course. When she was alone she would remember how he had looked and sounded, even the touch of him, although only his eyes had touched her, and she would shake inside.

But Maybelle couldn't know this. Now she said, 'We'll go through my appointments for the next few weeks and show him how far I'll be driving and tell him how useful you would be.'

'We're wasting our time,' Robin said, and then asked, because she was curious, 'If you're the one who's getting a companion why does it have to be his say-so?'

'Because Marc's the boss,' Maybelle Myson replied cheerfully.

She was a thoroughly modern woman in all but age but Marc Hammond made the rules, although it was a tender bullying Maybelle Myson got. He thought she should be kept safe from the likes of Robin Johnson. But it would be his fault if Maybelle went on turning down the other applicants and driving herself. She was a menace on the roads and before Robin left here she would tell him that.

'Your legs are younger than mine,' said Maybelle. 'Would you go downstairs? Through the first door on your left as you come into the house there's a bureau, and in the top drawer of that, right on top, you'll find a notebook with a red cover. Would you fetch it for me?'

'Of course.' Although going over Maybelle's appointments wasn't going to change Marc Hammond's mind.

Robin ran down the stairs. She would have liked to linger and look at the paintings. There was one of blue horses that made her pause for a moment but she wasn't on a sightseeing tour. The door was ajar and this looked like a dining room, dominated by a long oval mahogany table with chairs around it—lovely antique stuff—and a big carver chair at the head.

You could have a company board meeting in here, Robin thought, and she could imagine Marc Hammond sitting in the carver chair, the other chairs filled with folk, their faces turned towards him, drinking in every word while he issued orders and laid down the law. As this was a private house it was more likely that the dining room was used for dinner parties. Although Hammond would still be at the head of the table—as the host—the company would, instead, be guests having a wonderful time. He would be smiling and friendly and that was harder to imagine.

The bureau stood against the far wall, beside one of the long windows with their midnight-blue velvet curtains. It was smooth and polished in a warm, mellow wood inlaid with marquetry. She found the red-covered book in the top drawer. Then she stroked the top flap of the desk, tracing the pattern with her fingertips. The workmanship was incredible. There was a rose, every petal in a different shade of golden wood, and she breathed deeply, almost savouring a perfume.

Then she looked up from the marquetry rose to the photograph in a silver frame on top of the bureau, and all the sensuous pleasure of stroking the rose went in a flash. Here was Marc Hammond again, his dark hair springing back from a peak, his eyebrows heavy. If he lived in this house whoe the hell would need his photograph around the place? Even if he didn't live here it wasn't a face you'd be likely to forget.

She took a step back and glared at it—and he was

looking straight at her, demanding, 'What are you doing in here?'

Only, of course, it wasn't the photograph asking. The man was framed in the doorway, coming into the room, and she was desperate to get away from him, out into the hall, so that she went in a rush and he caught her by the wrist as she tried to pass. 'Hold on,' he said. 'What *were* you doing?'

She had the appointments book in her other hand. All she had to do was wave that at him but he was holding her and when she jerked instinctively his grip hurt, and for the second time this afternoon her blood pounded in her temples, so that she dropped the book and raised a hand and was within a hair's breadth of hitting him across the face. For a split second his face swam in a red haze, but while she still had her hand held high her blurred vision cleared and she gritted her teeth. 'Let. . .go. . .of. . .me.'

He didn't let go. He held her wrist, but lightly now. 'Nice bracelet,' he said.

Of course he recognised it, and he thought she was wasting no time in cashing in on Maybelle's generosity. She started to say, I'm not keeping it, but his voice overrode hers. 'You didn't know I lived here?'

So it probably was his house. 'I did not,' she said emphatically. 'If I had done I wouldn't have phoned and I certainly wouldn't have turned up. I know you wouldn't offer me a job after you threw me out for being a danger to junior clerks. By the way, whatever happened to what's-his-name?' She remembered Tony's name but she drawled that instead, acting blasé, as if the whole thing were hazy in her memory.

Marc Hammond said, 'He's doing nicely, thank you. You might have done him a favour. I doubt if he's ever been in a fight over a girl since. You don't seem to have changed much. Still very much the firecracker.'

Even if she had wanted the job she would have blown it by now, but she said, 'You're not going to believe this but I can't remember the last time I lost my head, until this afternoon. It was quite a shock seeing you sitting there and realising what sort of treatment I'd let myself in for.'

He agreed, 'It was a shock.' He wasn't holding her now but he hadn't moved away. He was still too close for comfort, sending shock waves rippling up and down her spine. She picked up the book and told him, 'Mrs Myson asked me to fetch this for her. What did you think I was doing—rifling the drawers to see what I could find?'

'Something like that, from the speed you took off.'

She had panicked but she couldn't say, I was trying to get away from you because you scare me. She said, 'You grabbed me; I hate being manhandled.'

'Sorry about that.' He was not sorry. She could believe that he had never said sorry and meant it in his life.

'What's the book?' he asked, and she held it so that he could read 'Appointments'. 'Now, why should she be needing that?'

'Ask her,' she snapped.

'Showing you where she hopes you'll be accompanying her?'

She gave an exaggerated shrug and he said, 'She's stubborn as a mule. She's found something wrong with everybody so far, so how have you managed to get her demanding you and nobody but you?'

'We have red hair in common,' Robin said silkily.

'*What?*'

'She had red hair, didn't she?'

'Copper-coloured.'

'Not like mine?'

'Not in the least like yours. You could set a house on fire.'

'Is that a compliment?'

'Only to an arsonist.'

This was a crazy conversation.

'And hair isn't the only fiery thing about you, is it?' he said, and she shrugged again because there wasn't much else she could do. There was no point in saying again that today she had been at her fieriest and most stupid. But she had something serious to say before she went.

'You should make her have a driver because she shouldn't be driving herself. I was in a car just behind her a couple of weeks ago, coming out of the old airfield from the market, and you know how busy that road is at weekends, and she shot straight out into the traffic like a bat out of hell. I've seen her have near-misses more than once; she's heading for a serious pile-up.'

She thought his skin whitened under the tan as if she had struck a nerve, or a memory. Then he said, 'You've got a licence, of course?'

'Of course.' Was he considering her?

'I'd want to see it.'

'Of course.' It was a clean licence and that would surprise him.

'At least there'd be somebody around who could use a phone if she needed help.'

'I think I could manage that,' she drawled. She had forgotten she didn't want the job. Maybelle was a danger on the roads and Robin would never forgive herself if the old lady had an accident that she might have prevented. And she liked Maybelle; being her companion-driver could be fun.

Being around Marc Hammond would be far from funny, but when he said, 'Come on,' and led the way upstairs she followed.

Maybelle was still sitting on the sofa with her feet up. She seemed pleased when Robin and Marc walked in together, as if this had to mean they were getting along. Robin wondered what would happen if she told Maybelle, We nearly came to blows just now. My wrist could be bruised and I was halfway through a swing to sock him across the face.

If she had hit him Marc Hammond would probably have thrown her out of the house bodily, as he had chucked out Jack the biker three years ago. He might look like the well-bred gentleman—expensively dressed, impeccably groomed—but Robin was convinced that he could turn in a flash into the toughest street fighter she had ever encountered.

'Thank you, dear.' Maybelle took the appointments book from her as Marc Hammond seated himself in a winged easy chair, his long body stretched out, strong hands resting on the arms. Robin sat down again on the little stool. He was relaxed and she tried to give the impression that she was too.

'Did Robin tell you why I wanted this?' Maybelle asked him.

'You tell me,' he said.

But he had guessed right and as she explained, 'To show you how useful Robin could be—I'll be doing a lot of driving,' he nodded. 'I think it was meant to be,' said Maybelle, encouraged. 'What were the odds against Robin arriving here just when I needed her?'

'It's a small town,' Marc Hammond said drily. 'The odds against somebody local seeing the "Situations Vacant" in local papers can't be that high. It's a slight coincidence that you've met before, but hardly fate taking a hand.'

Robin said nothing. Sitting low, fingers linked over her knees, the bracelet gleaming on her wrist, she waited for what Marc Hammond was going to say next, because now he was looking at her. 'Another thing,' he said. 'I would prefer this to be a living-in arrangement; how would you feel about that?'

'That would suit me perfectly.' She had expected to go from here to call on a friend and ask her for a bed for the night. A living-in job would solve that problem. Even with the prospect of Marc Hammond being under the same roof.

'When could you start?' Maybelle was taking this conversation as Marc's grudging consent and was anxious to get everything settled.

'Right away,' said Robin.

'Today?' That was fine by Maybelle.

'Yes,' said Robin.

'Where have you been living?' Marc asked.

He hadn't thought she would want to live in, on duty twenty-four hours more or less, and her enthusiastic response had increased his misgivings. He noticed that Robin didn't answer at once.

Her tongue licked her lips as if they were dry and it was Maybelle who said, 'Robin lives with her aunt and uncle. She has done since she was very young.'

'And now she wants to leave?'

Why not? Nearly everyone left their childhood home. And Robin said, 'Well, yes, I think it's time I did,' and smiled at Maybelle because she had a sick-

ening feeling that if she met Marc Hammond's piercing
eyes he would know what had happened this morning—every move, every word. 'I'm twenty,' she said.
'Don't you think it's time?'

'Twenty today,' said Maybelle. 'It's Robin's birthday, so isn't this a red-letter day?'

'There's another coincidence,' said Marc. 'And that,
I presume, is a birthday present.' He meant the bracelet, and he probably thought she had lied about her
birthday so that the old lady would find something
pretty, and possibly valuable, to give her.

'Want to see my birth certificate?' Robin asked with
heavy sarcasm.

'Not at the moment,' he said blandly, and Maybelle
hastily changed the subject.

'And Robin is staying.' Marc wouldn't go back on
that now.

'That is how it looks.' He was reluctant but resigned.
'I'm not happy about the situation; you both know
that. I don't consider her suitable.'

This time Robin glared back at him and wished she
could say, And I don't want any job where there's a
risk of coming into contact with you. But she did want
the job—for practical reasons and because she liked
Maybelle, and there was satisfaction in getting the
better of Marc Hammond. Deep down he must be
fuming at the idea of the wild child he'd thrown out of
his offices moving into his home.

It wouldn't last, of course, and that was what he was
implying when he said, 'But I'll give you the benefit of
the doubt for now.' He meant he would be waiting for
an excuse to dump her again. And something probably
would happen because something usually did.

Robin heard herself laugh scornfully. 'You won't

give me the benefit of the doubt. You were against me from the first day I was working for you, before there was any trouble at all. All you said was "Good morning; I hope you'll be happy here," but I knew what you were thinking.'

He almost laughed himself. 'You're right,' he said. 'You're sharp enough, I'll grant you that. I thought, We've got a time bomb here—and a few days later there was blood on the floor.

'As I've already said, you don't seem to have changed. You're still trouble on a short fuse and there had better be none of it around Maybelle. So watch it, Miss Robin Johnson, because I shall be watching you and I rarely miss a trick. . .'

CHAPTER TWO

ROBIN said, 'Fair enough.' It wasn't fair that Marc
Hammond should turn up when things could have
been fine without him, but that was life.

'So I'll leave you to it,' he said, and uncoiled himself
out of the winged armchair, and once he was out of
the room Robin felt her spirits rising and her strained
smile become relaxed and real.

Maybelle Myson's smile was gleeful. 'We've done it,
haven't we? Isn't this splendid?'

'Isn't it just?' said Robin. She would be out before
long—he'd see to that—but for now it was an enjoyable break for both of them.

'First of all, your salary.' Mrs Myson named a figure.
'Is that all right?'

'Great. Yes, thank you,' said Robin. It was very fair
indeed, especially as she would be living in, and, it
seemed, she was living in starting now, because Mrs
Myson asked her if she wanted to stay tonight and she
said, 'Yes, please.'

'You'll have to let your family know.'

'I'll phone,' Robin said, although she couldn't speak
to Aunt Helen yet and Aunt Helen always answered
the phone.

They went through a few pages of the appointments
book. 'Not much tomorrow,' said Maybelle. 'I have to
go to an animal-rescue centre in the morning. The rest
of the day's free. I've some friends coming round in
the evening.'

She seemed to lead a full and pleasant life; Robin had been mistaken in wondering if she might be lonely. She had plenty of friends, but at her age someone should be seeing that she didn't overtire herself, put too much strain on her heart.

I could do that, Robin thought. I'd have loved a grandmother like you. I could take care of you if he'd let me.

When it began to grow dusky Robin switched on a lamp which bathed the room in a mellow glow, and suggested, 'Shall I take the tray down? Can I get you anything?'

'We'll have supper later, but perhaps a glass of milk.'

Robin carried the tray downstairs towards the back of the house, opening what looked like the kitchen door.

It was a big room, a model modern kitchen so far as equipment went, but also with an old Welsh dresser that reached to the ceiling and with a scrubbed-topped table. The woman called Elsie sat at the table and Marc Hammond lounged against a worktop on which a coffee percolator was bubbling away.

He had taken off his jacket and was in shirtsleeves with his tie loosened. His throat had the same deep tan as his face and Robin thought his arms and his chest would have too. She couldn't imagine his being pale and soft-skinned anywhere.

He was relaxed now, but the coffee looked black and bitter enough to fuel his brain while he worked all through the night.

'I'll take that.' Elsie jumped up and took the tray from her, quickly, as if she was afraid that Robin might drop the good china. She put the tray on the table and looked at Marc Hammond with beady, bright eyes.

'Nothing to do with me,' he said. 'She's Maybelle's choice.'

Elsie stared at Robin then. 'I've seen you some-where before, haven't I? I thought that when I let you in.'

'Around town, probably,' said Marc. 'She's a girl who gets noticed.'

'Are you an actress?' There was a theatre company locally.

'I shouldn't be surprised,' said Marc.

'No, I'm not,' Robin said.

'You're going to be driving Miss Maybelle?' Elsie was not happy about that. Her mouth was pursing into worried lines.

'That's the idea. And generally making sure that she behaves herself,' said Marc.

Robin waited for Elsie to ask, That who behaves herself? But Elsie only sighed deeply and said, 'Well, I suppose anybody's better than nobody. Miss Johnson, is it?'

'Robin,' said Robin, hiding a wry smile, and Elsie looked as if that was a name she could hardly believe either.

'May I have a glass of milk for Mrs Myson?' asked Robin.

Elsie took a glass from the dresser and poured milk from the fridge, enquiring as she handed over the glass, 'She's stopping upstairs, is she?' and when Robin said she didn't know the housekeeper went on, 'I'll bring her supper up in about half an hour; will you be staying?'

'Robin has been persuaded to live with us,' Marc drawled. 'She's taking up her duties right away. You will be moving in tonight, will you?'

'Yes, please,' Robin said sweetly, and thought, Is that meek enough for you?

'Well, I never,' said Elsie.

He held the kitchen door open and they went into the hall together, Robin carrying the glass of milk, he with a large cup of very black coffee. As he turned into the room where he had interviewed her she saw the papers on the desk and asked impulsively, 'You don't want any typing done or anything?'

'No, thank you.' He turned that down flat. 'Nothing on that desk concerns you,' he said.

Trying to show him she was not a dead loss was a waste of time. She knew the papers were confidential and she said coldly, 'I wouldn't be snooping.'

'You won't be getting the chance.'

He shut the door behind him and she said, 'I hope the coffee scalds you,' but not loudly enough to be heard through a closed door.

When Elsie arrived with a tray—soup and a little fish—Mrs Myson said, 'You've met Robin; you know she'll be staying with us?' Elsie said she did, and Mrs Myson pondered, 'Which room, do you think?'

'Next one along?' Elsie suggested. Mrs Myson was happy about that and Elsie took Robin along to the next door on the landing.

It was a pretty room—curtains, bedspread and wall-paper in co-ordinating pastel florals, and a small shower room leading off. The window overlooked lawns and what, in the gathering gloom, seemed to be a large garden. Elsie stood in the doorway and asked, 'Will this do for you?'

'It's lovely!' Robin exclaimed, and from Elsie's expression it was as though she had expected Robin to be less enthusiastic.

'Right, then,' said Elsie. 'I'll leave you to it.'

A couple of hours later Robin was back in her room. Mrs Myson kept early nights. She had found Robin a new toothbrush and produced a white lawn nightdress. Then she'd said goodnight and hoped Robin would sleep well.

With no luggage Robin was glad to find the toiletry basics of toothpaste and soap in the shower room. She had no change of clothing, no make-up except for a lipstick and a comb in her purse, and she would have to go back tomorrow and collect some of her belongings.

She showered and put on the nightgown and sat at the window in the darkness, revelling in a quietness that wrapped comfortingly around her like the big, fluffy white towel she was huddling in.

She hadn't phoned home. When Mrs Myson had asked, 'Is this all right with your family?' she had said yes as if she had made the call.

She didn't want to go back tomorrow either. Some time she had to, because all the little she owned was there. But tomorrow Aunt Helen would probably be waiting for her, and the next day, while Wednesday was Aunt Helen's bridge night. She never missed that. On Wednesday Uncle Edward would be home alone and Robin could say goodbye to him in peace while she packed.

Mrs Myson had said that tomorrow morning she would advance her a month's wages, and that would be enough to buy essentials and clothes to carry Robin over. Every day here, if all went well, Robin would be feeling stronger and calmer. When she went back there would be no screaming if she could postpone it until Wednesday evening.

Marc Hammond was walking in the garden below. There was just enough moonlight to see him, and this time his presence was no surprise. He was probably needing a breath of fresh air by now, and if it had been Robin's garden she too would have walked there alone at night, revelling in the silence and clearing her mind.

She was sure that that was what he was doing, coming slowly towards the house. She kept well back, watching the dark figure approaching in the shadows down there. If he walked right under her window she could drop something on him. A pink lustreware bowl of pot-pourri, on the window-ledge, would be just perfect.

She would have enjoyed that immensely, but it was only a glorious fantasy. He couldn't see her but when he glanced up at the house she almost fell back into the room, as though he could see in the dark, and scrambled into her bed, between the cool sheets.

If something did fall on him out of the sky she wondered if it would surprise him. Well, it would of course, but how much? Nothing much seemed to surprise Marc Hammond. Not much surprised Robin either; she was used to the unexpected happening around her. Half the time she didn't know why it happened, and most of the time she didn't know how to deal with it. He'd said that *she* was a time bomb, but of all the men she had ever met Marc Hammond was the one who seemed to pack so much dynamic energy that she couldn't imagine life would ever be calm around him.

The difference was that he could handle trouble. In court he had the reputation of rarely losing a case, of being a born fighter, a born winner. But he'd lost the little tussle with Maybelle today. A stubborn old lady had got her own way and that made Robin smile.

Just for a moment she hugged herself, her shoulders shaking with silent laughter. Then she sobered rapidly, because what on earth was there to grin at in having Marc Hammond lined up against her?

She knew where she was as soon as she woke. She had slept soundly and if she had dreamed she couldn't remember. But she remembered where she was and what had led up to her being here, and she was going to be so careful today. She wanted to keep this job, and from here on it wouldn't be Robin's fault if things didn't work out.

Elsie met her in the hall when she came downstairs. 'I take up her tea eight o'clock most mornings,' said Elsie. It was ten to eight now. 'There's tea in the kitchen and he wants to see you in the garage.'

'Marc?'

'Of course.'

What did he want with her now? He had agreed yesterday to take her on trial, and the trial had hardly started yet so she must still be in the clear, unless he had decided he couldn't have her in the house after all.

She had butterflies in her stomach as she went from the kitchen across the narrow passage to a door that led into the garage.

There was plenty of room in there for two cars. Furthest away was Marc Hammond's dark red Mercedes. The door of Mrs Myson's car was open and Marc Hammond stood beside it. 'You wanted to see me?' she asked.

'Yes. This is the car you'll be driving.'

Mrs Myson's, of course. He got in on the passenger side and leaned over to open the door for the driver, and she gulped. 'Am I chauffeuring you?'

He said wearily, 'You don't imagine I'll let you take the wheel with her until I've seen for myself how you handle a car? And I'll want to see that licence.'

She got in reluctantly. 'Of course you will,' she said. 'I wouldn't expect you to take my word for anything.' She must not snap. She must stay cool and speak civilly.

'Put it down to my lifestyle,' he said. 'I don't take much on trust.'

He would be a poor lawyer if he did, but this was personal, and, considering she didn't get that much practice, she was a good driver. She'd show him she could ferry Maybelle Myson safely and without fuss wherever she wanted to go.

She checked the controls. Five-gear manual; she'd learned on one of those. She was not as composed as she would have liked to be; she was slightly psyched up, so that her cheeks were flushed and she had to remember to breathe slowly.

She didn't have to look at him though. She would keep her eyes on the road and concentrate on her driving. He pressed the button to open the garage doors and she turned on the ignition, went into gear, braked in front of the garage and moved smoothly up the curved drive to the entrance. She stopped there to check the road. Morning rush-hour traffic was streaming past. It could be a little while before there was a safe opening and she sat, hands on the wheel. 'Which way?' she asked.

'Into town.' Good, she thought; it would be easier to slip into the traffic than to cut across it.

But suddenly she was hit by a staggering jolt of physical awareness of the man sitting beside her. Being in the same room as Marc Hammond was traumatic enough. In a car the nearness of him hit her so hard that she nearly reeled from it.

She was fiercely conscious of the length and the strength of his body. It felt as if he was leaning across her and it was his arm, not the seat belt, holding her down, his hand on her breast.

'Waiting for your favourite colour?' he drawled, and there must have been times she could have moved out if she hadn't been so poleaxed. There was a gap now and she fumbled the controls, jerking and juddering into the traffic stream, and she heard him sigh at that.

She was on a straight road, going along by the river, heading for the roundabout just outside the town, She kept a steady speed and a safe distance behind a red car, but she was gripping the wheel so tightly that her knuckles whitened. She imagined she could hear him breathing. She couldn't, but she could smell the faintest tang of aftershave that seemed to be going right to her head, and the heavy breathing was her own.

She tried to block him out but that didn't work. Just by sitting close to her, his eyes rarely leaving her, he was turning her into a gibbering wreck. She had never felt such an urge before to beg, Leave me alone. . .give me space. . .

'Elsie hasn't met you before, has she?' he asked her.

'No, I'm sure we haven't met.' She was surprised that her voice sounded nearly normal.

'Just seen you around and wondered who you are?'

'Maybe,' she said.

'She could have seen your photograph in the *Herald*.'

Approaching the roundabout, traffic slowed to a snail's pace, and she nearly bumped the red car in front. She braked just in time and stared stonily ahead.

Earlier this summer there had been a festival of sound and light in the old airfield—a three-day rave with enough noise and excitement to annoy some of the more conventional locals. And when New Age gatecrashers had turned up, and the police had had to deal with the hassle, there had been enough action to fill several pages in the local weekly.

Robin had gone along that day with friends, for the music. They'd paid for their tickets, danced and enjoyed themselves, and Robin, who was gorgeous to look at and a graceful dancer, had caught the eye of a press photographer. Although she and her group had been well away from the skirmishing her picture was taken and she hadn't realised that.

There had been no names given in the caption on the front page but there had been Robin Johnson, hair flying, making—in one of Aunt Helen's favourite phrases—'a right spectacle' of herself.

Everyone seemed to have seen it. Marc Hammond obviously had, and probably believed that Robin had been stoned out of her mind, although she had never touched drugs in her life.

She went very slowly round the roundabout. She wasn't driving well but she was taking special care, and she had enough spirit to enquire tartly, 'Do you keep my press cuttings?'

There was only that photograph but it sounded blasé, and he said, 'If I'd known Maybelle was going to take this unaccountable fancy to you I might have done. Or at least followed your progress. It wouldn't

have been difficult. You must stand out wherever you
go.'

So do you, she could have told him. I've seen you
when you haven't seen me, and got out of the way
before you looked round because you always make me
want to run.

They were in the high street now and she asked,
'Shall I drop you at the office?'

She wondered who would remember the few days
she'd worked there when she drew into the car park to
put Marc Hammond down, but he said, 'Go onto the
motorway.'

'How far are we going?'

'I'm not abducting you.'

It was nerves that made her gulp, 'No danger of that
while I'm at the wheel.'

He said drily, 'No danger any time.'

He made her feel stupid. She couldn't rid herself of
the stress that was turning into creeping paralysis, so
that, by now, she was driving like a nerve-racked
learner. All through town cars were jostling for
position, slowing down as passengers jumped out, then
gaining speed again, all in fits and starts, and her hands
and feet were clumsy. She could feel sweat on her
forehead, and the palms of her hands were slippery, as
he sat beside her, saying nothing, not even in body
language, when she screeched a gear change.

She had driven through this town and manoeuvred
slickly with the rest of them. She had never had an
accident. But this morning she was waiting for a crash
to happen, and yet she was supposed to be a natural
driver.

Uncle Edward had taught her. Not in this town,
where they might have been recognised, but waiting

for Aunt Helen to be out of the way then driving to other towns, like conspirators, with Robin tucking her hair under a headscarf, giggling while she did it.

Uncle Edward had got her through the test and since then she had driven him sometimes when he was alone, and had driven friends' cars. She loved driving. Well, she had done until this morning, but this trip was drawn-out torture.

Somehow she managed to get through town and onto the motorway without scraping Mrs Myson's car. She was going by the book, trying to pretend it was her driving test again, although with Marc Hammond in the seat beside her it felt more like that old Arabian tale—the executioner with you while you carried a brimming chalice through the streets. One drop spilt and you were dead. One wrong move and the chop.

She stayed in the slow lane for just over a mile and she thought, At this rate this could go on for hours. She enjoyed speed and she *was* safe at the wheel. She pulled out when she could, and she put her foot down, and the engine purred as she took them up to the legal limit.

But she was still jumpy, and when a box shifted on the seat behind she half turned her head. The car swerved slightly and a driver alongside gave a furious honk on the horn.

Marc put a quick, steadying hand over hers on the wheel and said, 'Let's live,' and she jerked as if she had been burned. Then she snatched her hand from his and the words shot out.

'Oh, God, you make me so *nervous*.'

'I wonder why?' he said, but it was because he crowded her, knocking her off an even keel, and that was something else that was not fair. 'Turn at the next exit and go back,' he said, and she was so sure she'd failed the test and had nothing more to lose that there was an immediate improvement in her driving.

It was not up to her usual standard but she was giving an adequate performance and he said nothing. Neither did she, until she was driving into the garage. Then she said, 'Do I get a little list telling me why I've failed?' as if she didn't care, although, of course, she did.

'No,' he said, 'but don't put in for your advanced test.' That was nearly a joke. 'I suppose you're better than she is. Not that that's saying much.'

He wasn't sending her packing yet, although he was rating her pass a very near thing. She got out of the car as he climbed into the Mercedes and drove smoothly away up the drive, stopping to check the road. She stepped outside before the garage doors closed and she watched him now, and thought how she would love to hear a good loud thump and crunch when he did turn out of the drive. It didn't happen, of course, and, shut out of the garage, she went through the side-gate to the back of the house.

It was a big garden—a wilderness tamed and tended, the turf cropped to velvet softness, flowers in irregular beds, trees growing in a copse. She would almsot have worked here for nothing to have had the freedom of this garden, with the old red-brick wall around it and the seat under the horse-chestnut tree.

The back door led into the kitchen, where Elsie was sitting at the table with a man about her own age and a younger woman. The man had a mug of tea, the women had willow-pattern cups in front of them, and Elsie said, 'This is Robin. She's going to drive Miss Maybelle around. Morag and Tom.'

Tom looked like a gardener and Robin said, 'That is a beautiful garden.'

'Aye,' said Tom.

'She's in the breakfast room,' said Elsie. 'She said to tell you as soon as you got back. Been with Marc, have you?'

'Yes,' said Robin. If it had been less of an ordeal she would have said he had been checking her out as a driver, but she had made such a mess of that that she didn't want to talk about it.

'First door down,' Elsie said, and as she went out of the kitchen Robin saw them all lean forward, putting their heads together, and she was sure they would all start talking about her.

Mrs Myson was sitting at a table near a window overlooking the garden. She had two opened letters and she looked up, smiling, as Robin walked in. 'Tea or coffee?' she said.

'What have you got?'

'Tea.'

'That would be nice.' The cups and pot were here. There was muesli, toast, marmalade, and that was fine. Anything would have been good with the garden out there and Mrs Myson sitting opposite instead of Aunt Helen.

As she sipped tea Robin said, 'I've just had a driving test. He wanted to be sure I was safe.'

'I'm sure you passed with flying colours.'

'I only just passed. I really am quite a good driver but I didn't do so well this morning. I was nervous.'

Mrs Myson seemed to understand that. 'Marc can be overpowering and he is a very good driver himself. He's a rally driver.' It wouldn't have surprised Robin if he'd been a racing driver. 'He pilots a plane too,' said Mrs Myson.

Robin said gaily, 'He must take some keeping up with. How do his girlfriends manage?' She wasn't really interested, just joking.

Mrs Myson's eyes danced. 'Often they don't, but they try, my dear, they try.' Her laughter was infectious and Robin laughed with her.

After breakfast, with Mrs Myson in the passenger seat, Robin was an excellent driver. She judged her speeds, foresaw other drivers' antics, gears slipped in smoothly and she even found parking spaces.

The first stop was the cat rescue centre, home of the woman who ran the accounts, to deliver a box of tinned cat food. Mrs Myson stayed in the car while Robin knocked on the front door and handed in the box to a plump woman with a pussy-cat smile.

'This will be very welcome,' said the woman, and waved to Mrs Myson, sitting in the car at the kerbside. 'Thanks ever so much,' she called, and said to Robin, 'She's a wonderful woman.'

'I think so,' said Robin.

After that she drove Mrs Myson around the country lanes until lunchtime, when they stopped at a thatch-roofed pub called the Cottage of Content. Neither had been there before but the name was inviting, and inside there were dark beams and white ceilings and walls, and they had a very good vegetable soup and fluffy omelettes.

When they'd finished their coffee Robin asked, 'Do you want to go home now?'

Mrs Myson shrugged. 'I suppose so, unless you've any other suggestions.'

'Well, I would like to do some shopping.' She had a

month's wages in advance in her purse. 'I need some make-up, and I thought, perhaps, a dress.'

'What a good idea,' said Mrs Myson. 'Broadway has some nice shops; we'll go there.'

As they left the dining room more than one head turned to watch the tall, aristocratic old lady and the tall, beautiful girl.

They took their time wandering up and down the main road of the tourist town. They stopped to look into windows of antiques shops, art galleries, up-market boutiques. Robin bought inexpensive make-up, undies and a T-shirt, then spotted a dress that seemed reasonably priced in a window and asked, 'What do you think?'

'Let's see it,' said Mrs Myson.

It was just what Robin wanted—simple and stylish, drop-waisted, a perfect fit that rested lightly on her hips, in a silky material in a coppery shade. In the same shop she bought a pair of low-heeled black patent leather pumps, and when she went to pay was told that Mrs Myson had done so already.

This had to stop. After the bracelet this was all it needed to convince Marc Hammond that Robin was a grabber. She said, 'Oh, *no!*' but Mrs Myson had already left the shop and the car was only a few minutes away.

Robin said, 'I can't let you do this,' when she caught up with her. 'I must pay myself.'

'We'll talk about it later.'

Later Robin would hand over the money to Mrs Myson and say thank you, but it was getting late and high time that Robin was driving her home. In the car Robin asked, 'Are you all right? This hasn't been too much for you?'

'I've really enjoyed myself,' said Mrs Myson. 'Some very enjoyable things have happened to me this afternoon. In the dress shop the manageress said to me, "What a pretty girl your granddaughter is."'

'Oh!' Robin found herself blushing. 'I'm sorry.'

'I was flattered.' Mrs Myson laughed delightedly. 'And when we were walking along almost every man we passed turned to look again. I saw them reflected in the windows.'

'Oh, that,' said Robin.

'You're used to it,' Mrs Myson teased, 'but it's a long time since it happened to me. Women always turn and stare when I'm with Marc but today the men did, and if they thought I was your grandmother perhaps they thought, That's where she got her good looks from.'

Robin suspected that the old lady was talking nonsense to stop her arguing about the bill in the dress shop, but it was fun, and although Robin was determined to settle that account later the journey passed in listening to a chat show on the radio, with Mrs Myson saying every five minutes or so, 'Don't they talk a load of rubbish, these politicians?'

The Mercedes was in the garage when Robin backed her car in. 'Marc's home,' said Mrs Myson happily, and all the fizz went out of the day for Robin. The door from the garage going into the side-passage was unlocked, and they came into the house through the kitchen.

'We're home,' Mrs Myson called, and Elsie came down the stairs at the same time as Marc Hammond came into the hall.

'You haven't been overdoing it?' Elsie sounded accusing and Mrs Myson smiled.

'We've had a lovely time. We went shopping in Broadway.'

'So I see,' Marc Hammond said wryly. Robin was carrying two large red shiny bags with 'Sandra's' in black flowing script across them. 'Not for you, I imagine.'

'For Robin.'

'Of course they're for Robin. Who paid?'

'Marc!' Mrs Myson sounded as shocked as Robin felt. Then she went on to explain, 'Robin needed something to wear this evening.'

'What's happening this evening?'

'I've friends coming in.'

'And she has nothing suitable?'

Robin had no idea what kind of evening lay ahead, nor what she would be expected to do, but she wished desperately that she could have said, Of course I paid. Saying, I'm going to, was not the same thing at all. She would have said nothing if he hadn't been waiting for her to answer.

Then she had to admit, 'I don't have a change; I didn't bring anything with me.'

'You travel light. Is what you stand up in all you've got?'

'Of course not. I just haven't got round to collecting my things.'

'Then I suggest you do.'

'I will. But my old home's a few miles away.'

'Do you want to take my car?' Mrs Myson said.

And before Robin could stammer, T-tomorrow, perhaps? Marc Hammond said, 'No need; I'll take you.'

He saw the flare of panic in her eyes although she lowered her lashes to hide it, and her, 'Please don't bother,' had a hopeless sound.

'No bother at all.' He took the packages from her hands and put them on the hall floor; her fingers were too nerveless to grip. Then he went into the kitchen, heading for the garage, and for a few seconds Robin stayed where she was.

Mrs Myson gave a little shrug and a little resigned smile, and Robin remembered her saying, 'Marc's the boss.' This time protesting would do no good—Marc Hammond was going with her. He must want to see where she lived, but if he stayed in the car she could be in and out of the house fast.

He was in the car now, garage doors open, and when she climbed in beside him he asked, 'Where are we going?'

'Lower Meon.'

He said no more after that and she sat with her hands clenched together, her spine stiff and straight. Having him so near was playing havoc with her nerves again, but this time she was not driving, and there was no danger of a pile-up because she was having no effect on him at all.

It was the evening rush hour but he negotiated flow and counterflow like an expert, which, of course, he was.

Silently she said, I hear your girlfriends can't keep up with you. What I don't understand is who the hell would want to keep up with you. Not me, for sure. I always have this urge, when I see you, to run like crazy in the opposite direction.

They passed the old airfield and came to the village and then he looked at her, an eyebrow raised in silent query, and she directed him past the school, past the church, to the turning into the small estate.

'The third house down the road,' she said. Several

houses had cars parked outside but his would stand out, especially when it drew up outside the Hindleys' home.

At the kerbside she opened the passenger door and climbed out, and as he came round the car to join her she said, 'You don't need to come in.'

'You brought no references.'

'I can get you one.' They'd give her a reference at the last place she'd worked.

'Do that,' he said. 'In the meantime I'd like to meet your family.'

She pushed her hair out of her burning eyes. 'Like it?' she said harshly. 'If it's a character reference you're wanting, you are going to love this.'

CHAPTER THREE

IT SEEMED to Robin as though she was walking in slow motion up the short path from the gate to the front door. When the gate had clicked open she had seen one of the lace curtains at the lounge window fall back. Somebody had looked out as the car had drawn up, and it had to be Aunt Helen. She would be out of that room now, hovering in the hall, waiting for the bell to ring.

And if Marc Hammond thought Robin came from a wild family he'd be changing his mind as soon as he set eyes on the woman who opened the door, because Helen Hindley was always the picture of respectability with never a hair out of place.

This evening she was in a beige-coloured mid-calf-length skirt, and a twinset—jumper and cardigan—in the same ice-blue as her eyes. Her make-up was matt, a little heavy on the foundation, with pale blue eye-shadow and pale pink lipstick on her thin lips. 'Come in,' she said, and stood aside enough to let them into the hall.

Robin said, 'I've come to fetch a few things.'

'Well, I can't stop you.' Helen Hindley's fretful voice matched her expression. 'I've never been able to stop you.' That was not true but she made it sound as if it were.

'Is Uncle Edward in?' Robin asked.

'No.'

She would have liked to ask if he was all right,

because ill health dogged him, but she wouldn't get much of an answer, if any, and she would be back again the day after tomorrow to see for herself.

'I'll get a case,' she said.

As she ran up the stairs she heard Marc Hammond say, 'Good evening.'

The room that had been Robin's for most of her life was as plain and tidy as a motel's. Robin had always kept it that way because, given the slightest disorder, Aunt Helen would clear up after her and a tirade of abuse would follow that.

Now the bed was stripped. Aunt Helen had wasted no time after Robin had walked out. She was not expected nor wanted back, and now she took a case from a cupboard and began to pack at a feverish rate, anxious to get downstairs and get Marc Hammond away from here.

She tossed in clothes, shoes, toiletries and cosmetics, added her birthday cards, and left coats and heavy clothes for her next visit. Everything was rammed in and she sat on the top to shut the case and click the locks, then came downstairs fast, lugging the case down with her.

Aunt Helen had taken Marc Hammond into the lounge that was as cold and uncluttered as a furniture display in a shop. Robin wondered what he had made of that, what Aunt Helen had been saying to him. Aunt Helen was still looking martyred but Marc Hammond's expression gave nothing away.

Her aunt ignored Robin, but as she opened the door for them she said to Marc, 'Well, I hope she gives you less grief than she's given us,' and for a moment Robin hesitated.

Should she stand her ground and tell them both

what it had been like living in this house all these years, that the grief here was Aunt Helen, and that if Uncle Edward's heart ever did give out it would be because she had nagged him to death?

But it would have been a waste of breath. Robin looked at Aunt Helen and the older woman stared back unblinking, and Robin knew that Helen would have believed all she had told Marc Hammond no matter how wide of the mark or hurtful it was.

They were nearly out of the village before either of them spoke. Then Robin said, 'I don't want to hear what she said.'

'Do you sleep around?' he asked.

'*No!*' She almost screamed in his ear. She had guessed that Aunt Helen would have hinted at something like that, if she hadn't spelled it out. It was not true. It never had been. Robin had been blessed, or cursed, with the kind of sexy looks that made men lust after her, but even as a very young girl she had seen her power as a double-edged sword. It could hurt others, it could hurt her, and there was enough pain in the world without adding to it. She did not sleep around, and only within her own rules did she play around.

'So where did your aunt get the idea?' Marc Hammond enquired. His voice was lazy, idly curious, and she thought, I could never make you understand. I've never tried to make anybody understand. But she found herself answering him. Not looking at him. Staring straight ahead, seeing another scene in her mind's eye.

'She always expected the worst of me, but when I was thirteen I stopped wearing my hair in a plait. She'd always plaited it, right back, and so tight it used to

make my head ache. When I was thirteen I said I
wasn't having it like that any more. There were rows
galore but I kept it loose, and she said it made me look
a right little tart. She didn't need any more proof,
believe me.'

A deep line had cut between his dark brows. She
saw that when she gave him a sideways glance, and it
made her feel that perhaps he was understanding a
little.

Her voice lightened a shade, because now she was
saying something she had hardly realised herself
before. 'She doesn't know it but I guess she's been a
good influence on me, because every time she's carried
on as if I've got the morals of an alley cat I've thought,
You stupid woman, you don't know anything.'

He smiled at that and so did Robin. 'Did you tell
her that?' he asked.

'It wouldn't have helped. She believes what she
wants to believe.'

'So do most folk. You've lived there how long?'

'Fifteen years.'

'Why did you stay?'

After what she had just told him she knew it didn't
make sense, so she explained, 'Because of my uncle.
He's different.'

'He'd need to be.'

'We were in a hippie commune when my mother
died and it was my uncle who wanted to come and
fetch me, not my aunt. My mother was her sister, but
they didn't get on, and *we've* never got on; I've never
been anything she wanted.'

'She can't help it,' Uncle Edward had said of his
wife, a long time ago. 'Your mother got what she

wanted because she was pretty and always laughing. Helen got nothing.'

'She got you,' Robin had said.

And her heart had ached for the gentle, scholarly man when he'd said, 'And I'm no prize.'

Now Robin said, 'He has a bad heart and he seems to need me around.'

'But now you've decided to leave. Was that before you were offered a live-in post?'

'Yes, it was. I thought I'd have to stay with friends for a while. I do have friends.'

'I never doubted that.'

Was that said ironically? She couldn't tell what he was thinking, she could only wonder when she turned and really looked at the hawkish profile with the hooded eyes.

She said, 'Yesterday morning's row was a scorcher. It was my birthday, you know, and she's always remembered when I was born. My mother wasn't married and Aunt Helen never forgave her. Times might change but she doesn't.'

'Happy birthday,' Uncle Edward had said. Aunt Helen had started with a simple 'Ha!' then she had gone on about Robin's birthday being a black day, with the shame Robin's mother had brought on the family and how Robin was like her—'Born for trouble'—until Uncle Edward had walked out of the room. The way he always did. He loved Robin but he was no match for his wife and that morning Robin had reached the end of her tether.

'How he can stand living with you I'll never know,' she had stormed at her aunt. 'He's the only reason I've hung around all these years and I am leaving right now. I won't be coming back so that should make your day, and my mother might have been the wild one but you must always have been the bitch of the family.'

She had left Aunt Helen choking on that. 'I can't go back,' she said now.

'She isn't expecting you back. She seemed to know me, and when I said you'd be staying at my address, as companion to an elderly relative, she took it for granted you'd be living with me.'

'Well, yes, in a way.'

'As my mistress.'

'Oh, no,' Robin groaned; that was the way Aunt Helen's mind *would* work.

'She did warn me you weren't the faithful type, but she said you'd probably think you'd done all right for yourself this time.'

She said through gritted teeth, 'I am going to be sick,' and he grinned.

'That bad, is it?'

Yes, it was. It was mortifying, and she stammered, 'I—I'm sorry. That must have been so embarrassing for you,' although she couldn't imagine anyone or anything embarrassing him.

When he said, 'She's not the only one misjudging the set-up; Elsie was not convinced I didn't have designs on you,' her face flushed scarlet. 'She asked me if I was happy about the room you'd been given or if I wanted you in the one that connects with mine.'

So that explained Elsie's surprise when Robin had been delighted with her room. 'You did tell her?' Robin gasped.

'Yes, I told her. Don't worry.' This was amusing him and she decided that so long as he thought it was funny it could be a joke; it was ridiculous enough. 'Mind you,' he said, 'you don't look like a typical old lady's companion.'

'So I'm lucky that Mrs Myson isn't a typical old lady. Anyhow, appearances aren't everything.' She grinned cheerfully. 'You look a bit like Count Dracula but you're not, are you?'

'Only when the moon's full,' he replied, and she giggled. She certainly hadn't expected to be giggling coming back from Aunt Helen's, nor carrying on with such banter.

'You should have told Aunt Helen I was on approval. No satisfaction and I'd be dumped. Well, I will be, won't I?'

'That would have given her something to think about.' And they were laughing together at Aunt Helen, and Marc Hammond was, briefly perhaps, on Robin's side.

They were driving along the road past the old airfield, and she was watching the darkening countryside rushing past the window. 'I know you wouldn't have chosen me,' she said, 'and you're not thrilled that your aunt did, but will it be awkward having me live in?'

'Why?'

'Aunt Helen's just told you.'

'So she has.'

'People talk.'

'Are you worried?'

'I'm n-not, no.' She was stammering, getting into deep water. 'I thought perhaps you—'

'You think you might compromise me?'

That made her sound so stupid and so conceited and she said desperately, 'I thought that having a red-headed raver living with you—and that's how I look, isn't it?—might not do much for the good name of the old firm.'

'I think the old firm can stand it,' he said, and she still couldn't look at him. 'I don't need to reassure you, surely, that, seductive as you are, you are not going to be compromised by me?'

She was wishing fiercely that she had not started this. 'Oh, hell,' she said.

'Forget what other people may think,' he said cheerfully. 'We know what the situation is: armed neutrality.'

She was glad to be able to smile ruefully. 'You're the one who's armed and I'm the sitting duck.'

'A sitting duck should fit the bill nicely,' he said. 'Something quiet and placid and watchful. Only, that doesn't sound much like you.'

'Will you settle for watchful? I will watch out for her. Sorry you got such an awful character reference from my family.'

'Do you have any other family?'

'Only my uncle. No one else.'

She knew that Marc had a younger brother. Dominic Hammond was the junior partner, and even in the few days that Robin had worked for the firm she had learned that he was junior in every way. Marc was the dynamo. Dominic was popular and easygoing, but Robin hadn't noticed him around town after she'd left Hammond and Hammond and she had never given him a second thought.

'You've a brother, haven't you?' she said. 'How many more in your family?'

'Just Maybelle.'

They were reaching the roundabout now, where the

cars of those heading for an evening in town were
bringing the traffic almost to a standstill.

Robin remembered Maybelle and her wistfulness
and said softly, 'She said you were like a son but she'd
always wanted a daughter and a granddaughter.'

'I hope you're not giving her the impression that
she's found one,' he said cynically. Maybe he saw
something in her expression that made him add, 'Don't
even think of it.'

Before she could stop herself she snapped, 'Don't
tell me what to think.'

She could have bitten her tongue. The words had
jerked out just when the atmosphere between them
had seemed to be improving. The car was stationary
and he tilted her chin so that he was looking into her
eyes. 'That isn't an order, it's a warning,' he said. 'I'll
know what you're thinking if I have to get inside your
head to do it.'

She could almost believe he could. When she tried
to meet his eyes it felt as if he was reading her mind,
reaching the sudden panic in her. The car in front
moved and he took his hand away and looked ahead
and it was like being released from a force field.

She needed a few seconds to blink and swallow
before she could mutter, 'Remind me to wear dark
glasses.'

He smiled again then and she tried to smile too and
managed to keep quiet while they drove along the
road, alongside the river meadows, until they reached
the house.

In the garage she climbed out of the car and took
her case from the back seat, hauling it through the
door, getting it jammed so that she had to yank it. First

one lock sprang open then the other, and it burst open, scattering the contents around her feet.

She began grabbing them and tossing them back into her case, and she would have preferred it if Marc Hammond had not helped. Scarlet undies were great when she was wearing them but she didn't want them in Marc Hammond's hands.

The stack of birthday cards had fluttered out too, and he began to pick them up. 'I forgot my driving licence, but I do have one and no endorsements,' she said.

'I'd still like to see it.'

Then she said, 'Birthday cards. You didn't believe me there either, did you?'

He dropped the cards he was holding into the case. 'Let's say I have an open mind. Let's also say, Don't push your luck.' And he left her to her gathering up, his words echoing in her mind.

She must not push her luck. She must stay calm and careful and competent, because he was a long way from being on her side and he would come down on her like a ton of bricks if anything went wrong.

When she'd clicked down the locks she carried her case into the kitchen, hugging it in both arms to make sure it stayed shut. Elsie was there, taking a tray of little cakes out of the oven, and the smell was warm and spicy.

'Got everything you want?' Elsie asked, looking at the smallish case.

'Some of my things.'

'Shopping's up in your room.' Elsie put down the baking tin of cakes and began to lift them carefully, one by one, with the help of a broad-bladed knife, onto a wire-mesh tray. 'And she's resting. *Should* do

that in the afternoon. Remember that, will you, if
you're here to be looking after her?'

'That is why I'm here,' Robin said quietly, and Elsie
had the grace to look uncomfortable.

Then she said, 'I know that.'

Upstairs in her little room Robin wondered what
Marc had said to Elsie, assuring her that Robin was
here for his aunt's benefit not his. It shouldn't have
needed much stressing, only a few words like, Why
should I want the girl in a connecting bedroom? Don't
be absurd. She's an employee, nothing else, and likely
to be a temporary one.

Robin herself would have credited Elsie with more
sense. She seemed a down-to-earth soul and, surely,
knowing Marc Hammond as she must, she could see
that Robin was not his kind of woman? Just...not his
kind. Any more than he was a man Robin would ever
let herself fancy.

The shopping bags were on the bedroom floor and
she hung up her new dress, then opened the case and
began putting clothes on coat-hangers or into drawers.

She had seen Marc Hammond about town with the
kind of woman who would suit him—going into the
theatre, coming out of restaurants. And she'd seen him
several times in local newspapers and the glossy county
magazines—at social occasions, hunt balls. More often
she had seen him alone.

Elsie probably felt, as he did, that Robin didn't look
like a typical old lady's chauffeur-companion, and
perhaps she didn't. But she liked old folk, she got on
well with them, and it was fantastic that the old lady in
the ad should have turned out to be Mrs Myson.

She was lovely and there was a bond between them,
and if Robin wanted to pretend to herself that

Maybelle Myson was her grandmother how could anyone know? It was crazy, thinking that Marc Hammond might read her mind and know her dreams. Nobody could do that. He might have a maddening knack of blowing her control and making her flare up, but her innermost thoughts were safe from him.

When everything was put away she stripped off, showered, then changed into a denim skirt and a white cotton top with her new black pumps. She made up lightly, brushed her hair, then went to peep into Mrs Myson's room.

Her rest over, Maybelle, elegant and very wide awake, sat on the sofa. When Robin put her head round the door Maybelle said, 'I've been waiting to hear. How did it go?'

'My uncle was out and Aunt Helen hardly said anything to me,' Robin told her. 'She let us in and I went upstairs to pack a case so she was left with Marc.' She twisted her fingers and pulled a face. 'She thought I was moving in with him. . .' Robin's voice trailed off and Mrs Myson began to smile.

'*You* living with *Marc*?' The thought of Marc Hammond and Robin together really tickled her. 'You and Marc! My goodness,' she chuckled, 'wouldn't there be fireworks there?' Robin laughted too, although she didn't think it was that funny, while Mrs Myson wiped away tears of mirth with a lace-edged handkerchief.

'It was good in a way,' said Robin. 'After that she could have said anything and he'd have taken no notice.'

'Silly woman,' said Mrs Myson. 'By the way, you don't have to stay in this evening if you want to go out and meet your friends. You have your own life to lead;

you don't have to dance attendance on me all the time.'

All Robin's friends would have been fascinated to hear where she was living and working, but she didn't want anyone bringing up Marc Hammond's name. It was almost as if under their questioning she might betray something, to herself rather than to them, that she did not wish to face.

She said, 'I don't want to go out tonight. Isn't there anything I can do? Filing? Typing?'

Mrs Myson was delighted. 'You can type?'

'Yes.'

'We must get a typewriter.' She considered for a moment. 'If you're sure, you could do some filing for me. Well, some sorting out.'

Five minutes later Robin was opening the drawer of the bureau again, with the silver-framed photograph of Marc Hammond on top watching her. She put that face-down before she began to go through the contents of the top drawer. It contained a jumbled collection of letters and leaflets, invitations and theatre programmes, brochures and newspaper cuttings, and she began getting them as far as possible into order of date.

She had growing piles of papers on the long table when Marc Hammond passed the open door, did a double take and stepped back to ask her, 'And what are you doing now?'

'Sorting this lot out,' she said. 'Mrs Myson wants the bureau tidied.'

'I shouldn't think you can do much harm here, but hold on.' He turned to speak to someone. 'This is Robin Johnson whom I was telling you about.'

'Well, hello, Robin.' The woman with him had a

slightly mocking voice. 'I'm Leila Mannering.' She was tall and slim, with smooth blonde shoulder-length hair, wearing a beautifully cut cream linen trouser suit with a cream silk shirt, and carrying a cream patent leather purse.

Wherever she and Marc Hammond were going she would be a credit to him, Robin thought wryly, and the girl, who had been about to follow Marc up the stairs, stopped to give Robin a second and less friendly look.

Then she sauntered into the room, dropped her purse on a chair and, hands in pockets, walked a little way round the table, all the time eyeing Robin as if she were an interesting specimen, finally drawling, 'I've seen your hair around town.'

Robin was holding a two-year-old invitation to the first night of a ballet. She placed it in its date group and said, 'We get about a lot together, me and my hair.'

'And now you've moved in here, to drive Mrs Myson around and go through her papers?' Robin nodded and Leila rolled her eyes ceilingwards as if something up there might explain the situation. 'This has got to be positive proof that Great-aunt Maybelle is going gaga.'

'You should ask her about that,' Robin said sweetly. 'She'll tell you she's a long way from gaga.' And she knew that Leila was wondering if Robin might repeat this and how she, Leila, could deny she had ever said anything of the sort.

Leila need not have worried, but as she moved towards the door Robin said, 'Hey,' and Leila turned her head. 'Don't forget your purse,' said Robin. 'You can't trust anyone these days.'

'Nice bracelet,' said Leila. 'Haven't I seen it somewhere before?' Then she snatched up the purse and
stalked off, following Marc upstairs.

'Hold on', he had ordered Robin. Presumably while
he went to check with Maybelle if there were any
private papers in these bureau drawers.

Whatever Robin found, she could be trusted with,
and she finished emptying the drawer.

A few minutes later Marc came back to the doorway
of the dining room. 'Carry on filing,' he said.

'Nothing here I can damage, then?' She had the
table covered with papers. It looked chaotic but it
wasn't. 'Anything else?' she asked.

'It didn't take you long to irritate Leila.'

Robin shrugged.

'What did you say to her?'

'Nothing much.'

'"Nothing much" seems to have been enough.'

That was because Leila had disliked Robin on sight.
Robin could imagine her being charming with Mrs
Myson, but, coming down the stairs, she would surely
have said something to Marc like, Are you sure she's
to be trusted? and, Isn't that Maybelle's bracelet?

'If I irritated her in any way do apologise for me,'
said Robin tartly.

'Try not to ruffle any more feathers,' he said.

Robin had only given as good as she was getting, but
Leila's opinion might count against her with Marc.
Robin said, 'It—happens.'

'Just a flair for stirring it?' A corner of the long
mouth lifted and she thought she caught a glimpse of
fellow feeling. You and me both? she wondered.
Maybe, in that, we are two of a kind.

'Don't open the windows,' he said, and shook his head over the paper-strewn table.

She hadn't thought of opening a window—the air and the temperature were fine in here—but she asked, 'Why not?'

'It's getting windy outside. I can see you with all this flying everywhere.' Her lips twitched, and when he smiled the twitch widened to a grin.

'I won't open the window,' she promised, 'and I'll put everything back tidily.'

He took a couple of steps away then turned again. 'One other thing—you know Maybelle's got two old friends spending the evening with her? They may take to you; she certainly has. On the other hand they could wonder just what you are up to. Try to reassure them you're not planning on whisking Maybelle off on the travellers' trail.'

'You don't think I could lead her that far astray, do you?'

'Of course not.' He still smiled down at her. 'Because you know that if you put a foot wrong I would be after you.' It was a joke, she hoped as he went to join Leila.

She heard his car drawing away as she began to stack papers back in the bureau. The purr of the engine murmured in her brain and she imagined Leila's pale profile turned towards him. She wondered where they were going, what they had planned for the hours ahead. They were dressed for an evening out. He was as immaculate as ever in a dark grey suit, and she thought a table for two more likely than a dinner party or a gathering.

She wondered what the food would be, what they would talk about and, if they were lovers, how the saturnine face would soften, or if it would. She thought that with him even passion would be controlled, might even possess a hint of mockery.

She shut the drawer and stood looking at the silver-framed photo for a few seconds before she went out of the room, carrying the image of his face so vividly in her mind that he seemed to be standing at the top of the stairs, although she knew darn well he was not.

She went to her room and washed newsprint and dust off her fingers, then went down into the kitchen to ask Elsie if there was anything she could do.

'They're up there,' Elsie announced. 'And I've taken the tray in to them.' She smiled grimly. 'If she's told them she's taken you on they'll be wanting to see you and you won't be what they're expecting.'

'I've been told that a few times,' said Robin, but, as it happened, she was what they were expecting.

They sat, side by side, in matching armchairs, Maybelle Myson's contemporaries, wearing her kind of clothes, with greying hairstyles and discreet make-up. One of them was last year's mayoress, and although not a friend of Aunt Helen's was a woman who had know Helen Hindley well enough over the years to have heard some of her complaints about Robin.

Maybelle must have mentioned Robin's name, because they both looked at each other as she walked into the room. 'This is Robin,' said Maybelle.

And the ex-mayoress said, 'Ye-es,' as though her doubts were being confirmed.

They went on nibbling their cakes and savouries, as if this was a friendly chat over the teacups instead of a cross-examination with Robin answering the questions. One wanted to know how long Robin had been driving and if she had had any accidents. The other wondered what other jobs she had had.

'Robin worked for Marc while someone was on holiday,' said Maybelle. 'A few years ago. She was an excellent employee.' And her eyelid fluttered in a wink that only reached Robin and almost sent her into a fit of giggles.

If either of these two asked Marc he'd deny it fast enough, but it stopped the questioning, and they were soon into another topic far removed from Robin.

After a few minutes more she said goodnight and went to her bedroom. She hadn't riled them. She hoped she hadn't worried them. If Marc had any complaints it would be because she had let his name stand as her referee, but that hadn't been her idea. And she must stop thinking about Marc.

There was a small radio by the bed and she found a local channel and played it softly, curled up in her bed, letting the time slip by. Then she went to sit by the window and, with the lights out, looked down on the garden.

Nobody was walking there tonight. It would be her secret garden where she could walk alone. She crept downstairs and let herself out of the house, meeting nobody, crossing the lawns and wandering under the trees. There was a breeze blowing perfume in the air; some flowers must like the night. On the skyline was the pink glow of the town, and there was enough moonlight to see her way.

It was dreamy. She hummed a tune, and let herself drift into a languid dance as if she were wearing draperies that floated around her—just because she felt like dancing, all alone under the moon.

She wondered if Marc and Leila were dancing on the small, intimate floor of an exclusive nightclub. If his arms would be around Leila.

So far he'd touched Robin with a grip on her wrist hard enough to bruise and, tonight, the fingers holding her chin when he'd looked into her eyes had warned her. There had been no gentleness either time but he would not be like that with Leila, and Robin wondered how it would feel to be held by him in a dance. Or a caress.

She had stopped her lonely dance. She was standing still now, her arms crossed, hugging herself because suddenly the wind was blowing cold, and she hurried back into the house and upstairs.

In the hours that followed after the guests had left and Mrs Myson and Elsie must have gone to bed the house was quiet, but Robin was not finding it easy to sleep. She was as comfortable as she could ever remember being, in this pretty room in this super house, but she still lay tossing, listening to the sounds that came through her open window. Sometimes the wind howled, an owl hooted. There was the barking of a dog, the occasional car.

Not Marc's car. He was not home yet. She felt she would have recognised the sound of his engine and she was not hearing it, nor any movement in the house. He was making a night of it, staying maybe with Leila, and of course that was no business of Robin's, but something was keeping her restless.

In the end she switched on the radio, so low that it was a lullaby rocking her to sleep, because she had to get Marc Hammond out of her mind. She didn't want to think about him. She would hate to dream of him. She would see him quite soon enough tomorrow.

But Marc was not the Hammond brother she saw in the morning. There was no sign of Marc when she went downstairs, nor when she sat at breakfast with Mrs Myson, but his name came up when Robin said, 'Will your friends ask Marc about when I worked for him?'

Mrs Myson smiled. 'No, they don't see much of him and they won't start questioning him. They're dear girls, but they've always been worriers.'

She was still chuckling over that when the other Hammond strolled in. Dominic. Now that she saw him again Robin remembered him well. Cheery and jaunty with none of the controlled power of his elder brother. Marc was taller, leaner, darker, a self-contained man, whereas Dominic was a cheerful extrovert.

He came in with a wide grin. 'Morning, my love.' He kissed Maybelle's cheek and she smiled fondly on him.

'Have you come to have breakfast with me? Isn't Lucy feeding you these days?'

'Too well.' He patted his not quite flat stomach, his eyes on Robin. 'No, I've just dropped in to see the minder. I remember you.' He leered at Robin so openly that it was funny.

'I'm sure you do,' Maybelle said drily.

'And what I want to know,' said Dominic, 'is who's minding the minder?'

'Marc, I suppose,' said Maybelle, and Dominic swayed back in mock horror.

'You poor girl, I've had that; nothing gets past Marc.'

Robin had to smile. 'I'm not trying to get anything past him.'

'If you do, I hope you have better luck than I've ever had,' Dominic said. 'How about having lunch with me?'

'You mean both of us, of course,' Maybelle said

ironically. 'And the answer is no, we have an
appointment.'

'Can't win 'em all.' Dominic laughed and the two
women joined in.

When he'd left Maybelle said, 'Dominic's still a
schoolboy at heart. I don't know where the years go
with him.'

'And Marc?' Robin asked, and Mrs Myson shook
her head.

'It's a long time since Marc was a boy. I think he
was always a man. And Dominic's even right sometimes—not much gets past Marc.'

The morning trip was to a beauty salon in a small
neighbouring town, where Maybelle Myson had had a
weekly appointment for years. Robin walked round
town until it was time to collect her and they had lunch
in a hotel that was famed for its fish bar.

'Now,' said Maybelle, settling into the passenger
seat, 'I know where I want to go this afternoon.'

It was a little pilgrimage, to somewhere she had
visited with her husband, and it was a small miracle
because thirty years later it hadn't changed that much.
There was still a public right of way between the
houses, leading across fields up into the hills. They left
the car and Maybelle strode along, pouncing on way-
markers with cries of triumph and brushing aside
Robin's protests.

She was remarkably agile, but they would have to
retrace their steps, and Robin was getting anxious,
constantly asking, 'How much further?'

'Not far now,' came the reply, over and over again.

'Look, we have *got* to turn back,' she said finally.

'Nearly there,' said Maybelle, and she was away
again, but this time almost at once they were walking

between stones on the hillside. 'This was a nunnery,' Maybelle explained. 'A convent. Four, five hundred years ago. And somewhere around is the Nun's Well.'

Robin was never quite sure if they'd found the well, but among the rough grass and bracken was a small rock wall, broken into fragments, that could have been the top of a well, so she held Maybelle back and said, 'That's it; I'm sure it is.'

'Last time I dropped a pebble into the water,' said Maybelle, 'and made a wish.'

Earth filled it now, but it was the closest thing to a well they had come across, so Robin found a pebble and said, 'Toss this in.'

'Well, all right.' Maybelle tossed and presumably wished, and said, 'Now you.' And Robin picked up another pebble, flicked it after Maybelle's and wished that she would get Maybelle safely down to the car again without her spraining an ankle in a rabbit hole.

The light was beginning to fade, they had to go carefully, and Maybelle's stamina had peaked and was falling. She was as relieved as Robin to reach the car.

Robin should have given her wish a wider scope, wishing them home safely, because it was on the bleakest stretch of road that there was an almighty bang and the car went crazily out of control. Thank goodness there was nothing coming and no trees in the way as they swerved and screeched, ending on a grass verge just short of a ditch and the high, thick barrier of a hawthorn hedge.

Robin swore and so did Maybelle. 'Are you all right?' Robin gasped. They had been thrown around in their seat belts but Maybelle seemed calm enough.

'Knocks the wind out of you, doesn't it? But yes, I'm fine. You got us out of that nicely.'

Robin grimaced. 'We're not out of it. There's a tyre to change. I've never changed a tyre before but after this I'm going to learn.'

It was a far from busy road but there should be a car along eventually that would get them to a garage, Robin thought. Setting off walking would be riskier; Robin didn't know where the nearest house or phone was. 'Marc's been on at me to have a car phone,' said Maybelle, 'but I don't like the pesky things.' Robin switched on the hazard lights, opened the bonnet of her car to signal breakdown, and stood on the grass verge praying that someone would be along before it got dark.

It was almost two hours later before they got home, and as Robin backed into the garage Elsie came running through the door from the corridor.

'It's all right, we're all right,' Maybelle called through the glass of the car window. Robin had jumped out of her seat and hurried round to help Maybelle, who was moving stiffly.

'Where have you been?' Elsie wailed. 'Here, take my arm.'

Between them Maybelle walked into the kitchen and Marc's 'Where the blue blazes have you been?' was softly spoken but menacing. His anger was held in but Robin, not a girl who was easily cowed, quailed before it and felt her mouth go dry.

Maybelle sat down in one of the wooden armchairs and said, 'We went to the Nun's Well.'

'Sounds charming,' said Marc, still glaring at Robin, who wouldn't have minded sitting down herself but had to stay standing.

'We had a puncture.' Maybelle raised her voice, trying to get his attention. 'That's why we are so very late. It was a lonely road; we had to wait until a car came. The first one that did stopped to help us.'

'A male driver, of course,' said Marc.

Maybe Maybelle hadn't caught the sarcasm in his voice, because she said, 'A nice young man. He was very taken with Robin.'

He had stopped and might, in any case, have given them a lift, or offered to make a phone call, but it was after he'd really seen Robin that he had taken off his jacket and rolled up his sleeves, and, when the spare wheel had been put in place, had asked for her phone number. She had smiled and thanked him but said she didn't have a phone number, so he had written his down for her although, of course, she would never call it.

'Of course he was taken with her,' Marc said curtly. 'But personally I would prefer her to stop treating this job as a joyriding bash and show some signs of responsibility. It didn't occur to you to phone?'

He was still glaring at Robin and she tried to defend herself. 'There was no phone.'

'Marc!' Maybelle protested.

He looked at Maybelle then, and the anger went out of his face and his voice. 'You silly old biddy,' he said gently. 'You're not up to these games.'

And Maybelle did seem as if all this had been too much for her. Marc was right, Robin thought. She should have stopped Maybelle somehow, but she lacked experience in dealing with a really determined old lady.

'I think I'll lie down for a little while,' Maybelle said. 'If you'd bring me a cup of tea, Elsie. Robin, give me your arm.'

From someone who had been skipping up the hills

like a mountain goat she had become slow and shaky and Robin went to her side quickly. Marc had taken a step forward as if he would keep Robin away, but this much, at least, she was doing. She met his glare, scowling straight back. She could manage that for a few seconds but no longer.

Upstairs Maybelle relaxed on the sofa and Robin slipped off the old lady's shoes, hovering anxiously over her. She closed her eyes until Elsie brought in a cup of tea then she sat up.

'I've put in a drop of brandy,' said Elsie. 'You look all in.'

'Nonsense,' said Maybelle. 'But the brandy was a good idea.'

As she sipped Elsie said to Robin, 'And if I was you I should start packing.' At which Maybelle replaced her cup on the saucer so sharply that the tea sloshed over.

'I shall speak to Marc in the morning,' she said. 'I shall tell him it was not your fault we were late getting back.'

'Thank you,' said Robin.

But when she came out of the room Elsie caught up with her on the landing and said grimly, 'I should still start packing. You didn't see him before you got back. He isn't having any more of this.'

Robin did start to pack—not everything, but she put some of her clothes into her case and then she sat at the window for a while and hoped she could stay the night. Tomorrow she would start planning her life again, but for now her mind was numb, as if there would be no tomorrow and when she went away from here her life would end.

She had rarely been so depressed. She might have

stayed in this little room and kept away from Marc but it was still early evening, and if she could just escape from the house and walk in the garden she might find some peace there.

She came downstairs quietly and was tiptoeing past the open door of the drawing room when Dominic called, 'Hello,' and she turned slowly. 'Come in,' he said. 'What's going on?'

'Has nobody told you?' Marc, maybe—Elsie for sure, she would have thought.

But he only said, 'Marc's in a murderous mood; that's all I know.'

'And all I know is, I'm getting the sack. That doesn't surprise you, does it?'

'Sit down and tell Uncle Dom all about it,' he said.

'We were late back. We got a puncture. There's recklessness for you.'

'Ah,' said Dominic. 'Sit down,' he said again, and this time she did.

'Our parents were killed in a car crash,' he said abruptly. 'Lately Marc has intended making Maybelle take on a driver. Then she found you, and you are a lovely girl, my darling, but you do look a bit of a tearaway.'

She hadn't known about their parents. That was terrible—a tragedy of the times, which happened to so many families. She said quietly, 'I don't drive like a tearaway.'

'Perhaps you don't, but—' Dominic's boyish face tightened, ageing lines appearing. 'I was still away at boarding-school. Marc was waiting for them alone. Not here. We'd got a weekend cottage in Wales then. There was no phone, no houses anywhere near. He waited for them all night but they'd crashed miles away. They weren't found till the next day. The car had burned out and he had to identify them.'

'Oh, God,' she whispered.

He said bluntly, 'So when Maybelle's car's on the road and hours late, and nobody knows where she is, it doesn't help Marc to remember that you're driving.'

The driving test he had given her wouldn't have reassured him either, and he already thought she was turning her job into a freeloading perk. She should have known about the accident, she felt, although if it had happened while Dominic had still been at school he must have been a very young child. But Marc would never forget the night of waiting for his family who'd never come home.

She could have been what was wanted here, but to Marc Hammond she was trouble, putting his stubborn and cherished old aunt in peril. She said, 'I'm sorry—about your folks.'

Dominic was sitting beside her on the sofa and she was sorry for him and for herself. 'Life can be difficult, can't it?' he said.

The arm he put around her was just a comforting hug and she let her head rest on his shoulder. He was right about life, and her, 'Oh, it *can*,' was heartfelt.

For a moment they sat together without moving, and as she raised her head Marc Hammond said harshly, 'For God's sake, break it up.' They sprang apart. Crazily she almost felt guilty, and Dominic certainly did.

''Strewth, you nearly gave me a heart attack,' he blustered.

The floor was thickly carpeted and Marc Hammond moved quietly for such a big man; Robin hadn't heard him coming. Now he said, 'Shouldn't you be getting home to Lucy?'

'All right,' said Dominic, 'we don't live in each other's pockets. And Robin isn't feeling too bright right now. She thinks she's got to start looking for another job.'

'So long as you're not offering her one.'

Marc Hammond's eyes had narrowed and Dominic stuttered, 'O-of course not. Wh-what could I—?'

'And don't go overboard with the sympathy either,' Marc drawled. 'Nobody need worry about Robin. She's a girl who'll never go short of an offer or a shoulder to cry on. But she's getting neither in my house.'

CHAPTER FOUR

ROBIN sat up straight and tried to look scornful, because both men were behaving ridiculously—Marc suggesting there was overfamiliarity in her sitting by Dominic, and Dominic jumping up and carrying on as if they had been caught in a steamy clinch.

Dominic was still stammering. 'The o-old g-girl is all right, isn't she?' Robin had seen how fond he was of Maybelle this morning, but he *knew* she was all right, otherwise Robin would have mentioned it to him. He was changing the subject, although Robin would have preferred him to say, Stop acting like a prosecuting counsel, there's nothing going on here.

Some hope, she thought. About as much as expecting Uncle Edward to square up to Aunt Helen. Why were the nice folk usually so helpless?

'She will be all right after a night's sleep,' said Marc. His glance rested briefly on Robin. 'And don't you disturb her again tonight.'

Robin would have loved to enquire what he thought she might do. Go in and suggest Mrs Myson went out on the town? Make a scene over her job and upset Maybelle? Apparently he didn't think she could be trusted to go into Maybelle's room without causing aggravation.

'I'll be getting along,' said Dominic. 'Chin up,' he said to Robin, whose chin was already so high that her throat muscles felt taut. 'See you in the morning, Marc; I'm in number three court.'

'Yes,' said Marc, who would know that because he'd know what *all* his staff were doing, Robin thought. And one employee was being struck off the payroll. Robin, with her month's wages in advance, had been here two and a half days. Two and a half days less than the last time she'd worked for him.

When the door closed after Dominic she wanted to run across and open it again and hurry out of the room, but although Marc Hammond was nowhere near the door he seemed to bar her way.

She could hear a clock ticking, soft and fast. Only it wasn't a clock, it was her heart, or a pulse in her throat, and she said, 'You want me to leave now?'

'That is what I would like.'

He wasted no words and no energy. Even in the kitchen when he had been murderously angry with her he had still been in complete control and she thought, crazily, that she would give years of her life to shatter his self-possession.

She had been going to say, All right, then, and go, but when she stood up she couldn't leave it like that. She had to jolt a reaction from him. 'Would it help if I cut my hair?' she said.

'What?'

She put her fingers in her mass of red hair, holding it back from her face. 'If I looked less flashy would you believe that I could be more responsible?'

'I doubt if it would make much difference,' he said drily, but this was communication of a sort so she went on.

'I couldn't stop her going to the Nun's Well; you said yourself she still thinks she could sail a raft up the Amazon, and she nearly outraced me up the hills.'

'What is the Nun's Well?'

'Don't you know?'

'Would I be asking if I did?'

Probably not, so she said, 'Somewhere she went with her husband years ago and thought she'd like to see again. We didn't meet a soul. It was an old well up in the Cotswold hills in the middle of the ruins of a convent from the Middle Ages.' She realised he had never heard of it before and said, 'I think we found the well. We found a bit of curved wall with grass growing all round, and we threw pebbles over the wall. She said she'd dropped a pebble in the water last time she was there and wished.'

'I gather she enjoyed herself?'

'Yes, she did, and she was set on going.'

Maybelle would have known that Marc would have said it was too tough a climb for her. She had conned Robin, and Marc seemed to understand that, because she saw the half-smile as he asked, 'What did you wish for?'

'You don't tell them, do you—wishes?'

'Something else I didn't know.'

'Mine came true, so I can tell. I wished I'd get her back to the car safely; there were a lot of rabbit holes.' She risked her first grin. 'I should have wished for no punctures on the way home.'

'That was bad luck.' He was sounding less of the iceman. 'You must have a mobile phone.'

He wasn't blaming her; he wasn't sacking her. She said breathlessly, 'I can stay?'

'You're one hell of a problem but that isn't how Maybelle sees it, and it seems this jaunt was her idea, not yours.'

'Thank you.' She was thrilled. With anyone else she would have at least caught a hand but Marc Hammond was untouchable, so she smiled radiantly at him and he looked back as if she puzzled him.

'I still find it odd that you want this job,' he said.

'Maybelle's exceptional—I know that—but I'd have thought you would have preferred faster, younger company. Why are you anxious to spend your time with an old woman?'

She couldn't tell him that she felt somehting like kinship for Maybelle Myson, that with Maybelle the age barrier didn't matter, because he thought Robin was too superficial to be able to appreciate that.

'I like her,' she said.

'And that isn't because you think she's a wealthy woman?'

All along he had believed she was taking advantage of an old lady's kindness, but hearing it said so bluntly caught her on the quick like the flick of a whip, and instinctively she raised an open hand.

In the same quiet tones he said, 'This is the second time you've felt the urge to lash out at me. Get a hold on yourself.' And she knew without any doubt that if she struck him he would floor her.

She threw the outflung arm into a wide gesture and put bite in her words. 'I paid for my shopping. I don't want anything for nothing.'

This morning she had insisted while Maybelle demurred, saying, *'Please,'* until Maybelle had sighed and smiled and given in.

He said, 'That would be the sensible thing to do.' Not to appear too grabbing, he meant. 'But, for your information, Maybelle's income is a long way off a fortune. There could be pickings if you stay with her, of course, but I'll make sure they're not extravagant and you can forget any idea of inheriting. All you can see—this house and more or less everything in it—belongs to me.'

Whenever she started to like him a little he acted in character again and she went right back to hating his guts. She might have risked getting knocked down for the joy of socking him if she hadn't known that he would grab her arm before she could get the first blow in.

She bared her teeth in a flagrantly false smile. 'The idea I'm here as a fortune-hunter is nearly as funny as Aunt Helen and Elsie thinking I fancy you.'

'There's not much danger of that,' he said, and when the phone rang and he went into the hall to answer it she thought, Saved by the bell, because Lord knew what she might have said next.

She heard him acknowledge the caller. 'Uh-huh.' Then he said, 'Don't you?' and, after a few seconds, 'Marginally.' Then he put down the phone and looked at Robin, who was standing in the doorway of the drawing room. 'That was Dominic,' he told her. 'On his car phone, because he couldn't wait to remind me that you couldn't help having a puncture and that you have to be a better driver than Maybelle.'

Dominic seemed to find it easier to stand up to Marc when he didn't have to face him. That was pathetic, but she was touched that he had spoken up for her. 'That was sweet of him,' she said.

'Yes,' said Marc ironically. 'He's sweet. He's also a pushover for a pretty face and you're the girl your aunt says is always leading the men on and letting them down. So leave Dominic alone.'

'That's more or less what you said about Tony.' She could almost imagine herself back again in that office, because the man facing her hadn't changed and the background didn't matter. And the way Marc Hammond had treated her then had been unfair too. She tried to mimic his voice. 'He "wouldn't stand much of a chance if you moved in on him" you said. I hadn't led Tony on, unless you count eating a sandwich with him after he'd pestered me all week as leading him on, and, as for Dominic, I could not be less interested.'

'Keep it that way.'

'Yes, sir,' she called after him as he walked away from her down the hall, and her voice in her ears sounded like that of a child trying to get in the last word.

She let herself into the garden and went blindly over the grass until she was across the long lawn and under the trees. Then she stood, arms folded so tightly that she was gripping her shoulders and with her head flung back so that the night air cooled her burning face.

That *bloody* man! Nobody else could make her this mad. First he called her a grabber. Then he called her a man-eater. And she could think of a few things she would like to call him. If she did have to leave here she would tell him exactly what she thought of him before she went. He must know her opinion but she would *tell* him what an arrogant swine he was.

She began to pace up and down, rehearsing in her mind everything she would like to say to Marc Hammond, starting with, I am not a man-eater but you're probably a womaniser; how long do they last if they can't keep up with you? and going on to an insult that she was almost sure was rubbish—sure *you're* not after your aunt's money? Why should you worry how she spends it if you're not planning on getting your hands on it?

This was almost as good for letting off steam as

slanging him to his face. She had been blazing when she'd started pacing. A few minutes later she was grinning. She looked back at the lighted windows of the house and said aloud, 'And I wouldn't fancy you if you were the last man on earth.'

She felt better for that. Being all alone out here in the peace of the garden had been as healing as any shrink's couch, helping her get things in proportion again. The main point was that she still had the job, and she wanted to stay where she could walk in this garden and Maybelle Myson was her friend.

She was too independent to cadge, so Marc Hammond wouldn't get her there, and she would take great care not to give Dominic wrong ideas. He was pleasant enough but he didn't turn her on, and even if he had she would have kept her distance. Lucy had to be either his wife or live-in partner and Robin didn't poach other girls' men. She had never needed to; there were always enough of the free and willing around.

When she came back into the house and glanced at her watch she coud hardly believe it was only half past eight. The past few hours seemed to have lasted a long time but a good part of the evening was still ahead of her. Mrs Myson would be resting and nobody else in this house wanted her company. She could watch television or she could go up into her room and listen to the radio. Or she could go in to town and join some of her friends.

To heck with being ordered not to look in on Maybelle again; Robin wouldn't be easy until she had seen for herself that the old lady was all right. She went upstairs and opened the door quietly. There was no one in the sitting room but the bedroom door was open and Maybelle Myson sat up in bed, pillows piled behind her, reading a large-print novel.

There was nothing wrong with her hearing. She heard the door open and she called, 'Come in.'

'All right?' Robin whispered.

'Perfectly all right.' She looked fine. 'How about you?'

'I can stay, I think,' said Robin, and Maybelle gave a little satisfied nod.

'Well, I knew you could.'

'I thought I'd go into town for an hour or so,' said Robin.

'Take the car.'

It was just over a mile along the road. Robin could walk or hitch, and she smiled and said, 'I daren't chance it. After today I'd be scared of running into a tree or somebody running into me.'

Maybelle laughed, 'Well, if you feel like that... Anyway, take my key; it's in the bag by the sofa. We'll have to get you one cut.'

As he would to her using Maybelle's car tonight Robin felt sure that Marc Hammond would object to her being provided with a key to his house. She was pretty sure he wouldn't want her rummaging through Maybelle's handbag either, so she carried that into the bedroom.

Maybelle tipped it up on the quilt and came up with her house key from among a mass of handbag clutter and a couple of rings set with glittering stones. One looked like a half-hoop of diamonds, the other a big, square-cut emerald.

'Are those real?' Robin gasped.

'Of course.'

'You shouldn't be carrying them around like this. You could lose them; you could get your bag snatched.'

'Oh, I shouldn't think so,' said Maybelle blithely, turning a page of her novel.

Tomorrow, thought Robin, I must get her to leave them at home, or I won't dare take my eyes off that handbag. She might mention it to Elsie. She could not say anything to Marc; he would be asking why she was concerning herself with Maybelle's jewellery and if the bracelet wasn't enough.

She left the house by the side-door and five minutes down the road a car, with two of her old mates in, picked her up. She had known Emma and Chris since her early teens and spent many an evening with them, often in the riverside pub that they were making for now.

The Boathouse was a favourite. Tourists usually packed the tables inside, but on warm evenings like this Robin's friends took drinks and snacks out to their usual stretch edging the tow-path.

There was a small crowd of locals there now and, as always, eyes followed Robin as she moved towards them through the strangers. She sat cross-legged on the grass, and smiled up at the young man who had brought her a glass of white wine.

'Thanks for the cards,' she said.

Several of them had remembered her birthday and a girl asked, 'Have a good birthday?'

'So-so. I had the biggest and best row yet with Aunt Helen and got chucked out.'

They had expected that for years. 'Where are you staying?' the young man who had bought her wine asked, and got a sharp look from his girlfriend, who hoped he wasn't going to suggest Robin stay with them.

'I've got a job,' said Robin. 'With a Mrs Myson, driving her around and doing some secretarial work and living in. A house on the Liddington Road.'

Very nice, they all thought. Those were big houses; who else was there? they asked. She said, 'A house-keeper, and there's a gardener and a girl who comes in.' And she waited for someone to ask, Isn't Mrs Myson related to Marc Hammond, the lawyer?

But nobody said that because none of them knew.

They could soon find out whose house it was, but for now Mrs Myson was just a well-off old girl who had found Robin a job. And Robin said, 'I don't suppose I'll be there for long,' so neither Mrs Myson nor the job seemed particularly interesting to them.

Marc Hammond would have interested them. If they had known to what extent he was occupying Robin's mind, as she sat talking and joking with them, they would have been staggered. To Robin he seemed more real than they did, as if she could have touched him by reaching out a hand, while the little chattering group were just background shadows.

It was bright and cheerful here, after dark in the summer. The lights from the town and the shop windows streamed down the roads leading to the river, riverside cafés and small hotels twinkled with multicoloured fairy lights, and across the water the theatre was spotlit, with a full house and a full car park.

In the car park a year ago she had seen Marc Hammond get into his car. He hadn't noticed her—she had been with a couple of friends, heading for their car—but she had watched him climb into the Mercedes and drive away.

She had seen the car other times, around town, and had always recognised it. Just as she always recognised him, spotting him in the street going into and coming out of buildings. In crowds he was the tall man, but it was as if she had some sort of radar that homed in on him anyway, so that she sensed where he was—or even where he was going to be, because more than once she had stared at a doorway just before he stepped out of it.

So many times, and she could remember them all. In her mind she went around the town, ticking off her sightings. How many? She changed the poet's line to, When did I see thee, let me count the days... Although, it couldn't have been further from Elizabeth Barrett Browning's, 'How do I love thee? Let me count the ways.' That made her grin, so that she had to pretend to be laughing at a joke someone had just told and she hadn't heard.

When the Boathouse closed some of them were going back to a house, to play music, talk and drink, do whatever they fancied, but Robin was not joining them. She said, 'I have to get back,' and when she was offered a lift she said, 'Bless you.'

Andrew was a successful salesman. He fancied Robin and he fancied his chances, although he hadn't made much headway with her up to now. On the way home he kept up his sales patter, selling himself, but tonight she seemed miles away. You never did know with Robin, he thought, and tonight he hadn't a clue what she was thinking about.

She was thinking of all the times someone had given her a lift back to Aunt Helen's after an evening out, and how she had never much wanted to go back. Tonight was different. She told Andrew where to turn off the road, and driving through the gates was like coming home should be—giving a feeling of warmth and contentment.

She heard Andrew whistle—it was quite an impressive house—and she sat for a moment after the car drew up because she wasn't used to this sensation and it was pleasant. Then Andrew blasted the horn, shattering the silence with the force of a police siren, and Robin nearly jumped out of her skin.

'That got your attention.' There were lights on in the house and Andrew went on, grinning, 'Your old duck still seems to be up.'

'Shut up,' she screeched, and he took his finger from the button as she scrambled out of the car fishing frantically in her purse for the key. 'If that front door opens,' she panted, 'my old duck will be the least of your worries.'

She was at the front door before Andrew could say any more, and he had sense enough to realise that he should be leaving; he had done himself no good with Robin tonight.

The key turned in the lock and everything seemed quiet in the house. Marc was still up, of course. She knew he was before she passed the open door of his study, making for the staircase. He was sitting at his desk, papers before him, coffee at his elbow.

She had seen all that clearly almost before she turned her head when he spoke. 'Rowdy lot, your mates,' he said.

'Sorry,' she said.

She hurried for the staircase and Elsie, struggling into a dressing gown, was coming along the landing gasping, 'What's going on? Is there a fire?'

It might have sounded like a fire or a break-in alarm

to someone being woken from sleep, as Elsie obviously had been.

'It's nothing,' said Robin. 'A friend gave me a lift and pressed the horn by mistake.'

Elsie snorted and went into Maybelle's rooms, and Robin listened behind her own bedroom door, keeping it open a crack. Elsie came right out again, so Maybelle hadn't been disturbed.

Maybelle Myson had had a good night's sleep. Next morning all her energy seemed restored, but Marc had left instructions with Elsie that Maybelle was to have a quiet day. He hadn't seen Robin—he had left the house early—but he probably wouldn't have trusted her to obey an order. So it was Elsie who was in charge of keeping Maybelle resting, more or less.

Maybelle and Robin had breakfast together, while Maybelle opened her mail and they both glanced through newspapers. Then they went over Robin's filing in the bureau, consigning more than half the papers to the wastepaper bin and putting the rest back in order. Maybelle dictated a few letters and made a note to ask Marc for a typewriter.

They had lunch. After that Maybelle rested for an hour and then decided she could face being driven around the countryside. This taking-it-easy was rather a joke because she was in good health and spirits, teasing Elsie when she said she and Robin were going out in the car. 'For a nice gentle run—nothing exciting, just a change of scenery. We won't go near a town, I won't get out of the car, and we'll be back no later than half past six.'

'See you're not,' said Elsie to Robin.

Robin enjoyed the run and it was exactly what

Maybelle had promised—a leisurely spin along country lanes and through picture-postcard villages. They had music playing quietly on the radio, and there were comfortable silences as though they had known each other for years. When Robin got wolf-whistles at traffic lights, or from passing motorists, Maybelle would smile indulgently, as if she remembered when this had first happened to her.

They were back on time and they had tea in Maybelle's room. Tonight Robin was going to fetch the rest of her belongings and reassure Uncle Edward that she was safe and happy. He would worry until he saw her, she knew that, and if she tried to phone him at home there was always the risk that Aunt Helen might take the call or overhear it.

Robin would have preferred to go by taxi, but Maybelle tried to insist on her using the car, and when Marc walked into the room, just after seven o'clock, Robin had just agreed to wait until half past seven before she rang the taxi rank or if Marc came home first, to let Maybelle discuss with him her taking the car. 'I don't want him thinking I'm making free with anything,' Robin had explained.

As soon as she saw him Maybelle said, 'Marc, will you tell this girl I can do what I like with my own car?'

'Why?' he said. 'What is she suggesting you do with it?'

Robin nearly snapped, Trade it in for a red racing model to match my hair.

'She's collecting some more of her things from her old home,' Maybelle explained. 'And what is the sense in her taking a taxi when my car's sitting the garage?'

'No need for either,' he said. 'I'll be going that way.'

'I don't want you taking me,' Robin blurted out.

'Please yourself,' he said. 'But two cars rolling up together doesn't make much sense.'

'You're going there? Why are you going there?'

Robin didn't like the sound of this, and when he said, 'To see Mr Hindley; he asked me to call this evening,' She shook her head in bewilderment. 'I had a call from him this afternoon,' Marc went on. 'He wanted your phone number; I gave it to him. He rang here and you were out. Then he rang the office again.'

And got Marc Hammond again? Uncle Edward was showing a rare determined streak.

'I told him I believed he'd be seeing you this evening.' She had told Marc she woud be going back when Aunt Helen was out. 'And he said it would be a relief to him if I came along too.'

'What for?' Robin didn't need a meeting between Uncle Edward and Marc Hammond. They didn't have a thing in common, certainly not her, and the fact that Marc Hammond wasn't hiding his amusement didn't help.

Nor did Maybelle, smiling as she said, 'Aunt Helen has been talking. She does sound a very silly woman.'

'I think you're right,' said Marc. 'Your uncle wants to know my intentions. But he does seem genuinely concerned about you, and the least we can do is put his mind at rest. Tell him he's welcome to call here any time, to meet Maybelle and see for himself what the set-up is.'

'I can tell him that,' Robin offered eagerly. 'He knows I never lie to him and I'd love him to meet Mrs Myson.'

'I'd like to meet him,' said Maybelle, with a mischievous twinkle. 'So long as he leaves your aunt behind.'

'So you don't need to come with me tonight,' said Robin.

'I said I would,' said Marc, 'and that we'd be with him at eight o'clock.'

It would be all right in the end, because Uncle Edward would much prefer to know that Robin was working for Mrs Myson rather than living with an older and vastly more sophisticated man, for all Marc Hammond's success and status. But the first few minutes would be mortifying, and she could do without hearing Marc Hammond insisting that he had no personal interest in her whatever.

She got into the car with Marc, feeling as if she was going to the dentist. Her teeth rarely needed treatment and never anything drastic but she always felt queasy and she resented Marc Hammond for putting her through this. It wasn't going to bother him, but she was squirming with embarrassment already, and he need not have come. He could have made an excuse and she could have explained that too.

She had sighed deeply before she'd realised she was going to and he gave her that sidewards grin. 'It could have been worse,' he said.

'How could it?'

'Instead of phoning, your uncle could have turned up at the office. Miss Hodgkiss still mans Reception. He could have told her, I want to see Hammond; he's carrying on with my niece, Robin Johnson.'

Uncle Edward would never do a thing like that—he hated scenes—but the thought got a weak smile from Robin as she asked, 'Does Miss Hodgkiss remember the last time?'

'She's never spoken about it again. Neither has Tony, but they'll never forget it. Or you. There've been a few angry words exchanged in that entrance, but that was the only time blood was spilt.'

'A nose bleed.'

'A punched nose.' He laughed and so did she. 'Do men still fight over you?' he asked.

'They push each other around sometimes. The thick ones.'

'And what do you do?'

She thought about that. 'Now you ask,' she said after a few seconds, 'I lose interest. It's no joy being snarled over like a bone between two dogs.'

'So,' he said, 'even looking like a top model has its drawbacks.'

'Do you think I look like a top model?' She didn't know why she was asking him that, fishing for flattery.

'Come off it,' he said. 'You know exactly how you look. How old were you when you realised you were beautiful?'

That was a compliment, although he probably thought she was conceited and shallow. 'When I took my hair out of that plait,' she said, 'and began to wear it loose I started to feel better about myself. How old were you when you realised you were going to have a mind like a steel trap?'

'Nearly twelve,' he said.

They laughed together and she thought, This is a mad situation, Aunt Helen telling Uncle Edward that Marc and I are lovers. It's a joke; that is how Maybelle and Marc are treating it and I have to see the funny side too, because I must go in there and convince Uncle Edward how ridiculous it is. I shall say, I know what Aunt Helen's been saying and of course it isn't true. You know how she always comes up with the worst.

She wouldn't let herself wonder, even for a moment, if having Marc as a lover would be the worst thing that could happen or if it might be incredibly exciting. Even thinking about him making love to her was playing with fire. It would never happen, and if it did it would be for the worst in the end because he would burn her to ashes and blow her away.

'We're here,' he said.

'The old place doesn't change much,' she said brightly. 'Just the same as it was on Monday night except the curtain isn't twitching.'

And no one answered the door when Robin rang the bell. She rang again, keeping her finger on the bell push, then knocked, and called through the letter box.

'He should be in,' she said, which they both knew.

'You don't have a key?'

'Aunt Helen didn't trust my friends; she didn't like me having a key.' He might agree with Aunt Helen there.

'We'll try the back door,' she said. 'He could be on the phone or out at the back.'

There was no one in the patio of a garden and the back door was locked. 'Could he be at a neighbour's?' Marc suggested.

'He could.' He had friends around. 'But. . .'

'But you're worried?'

'He's got heart trouble. I'm always worried about him. I can get in.'

A thick, gnarled bough from an apple tree grew near an upstairs bathroom window and the small top window had a dodgy lock. Nobody else knew that. Not even Uncle Edward. Robin dragged off her skirt, babbling, 'I got out and in like this when I was locked in my room when I was young. I'm sure I can still do it.'

'It might be easier to break a window down here.'

But she was already swarming up the tree, clinging to the bough and easing the wooden window-frame this way and that until she pushed it open and swung herself up.

She went in, working her head and shoulders through, wriggling like a snake, her hair falling forward in a heavy veil until she squirmed through and landed on all fours on the thin carpet. Then she was out of the room in a flash, calling, 'Is anyone in? Hello? Uncle Edward?'

She opened bedroom and bathroom doors, and the rooms were empty. Running downstairs, she raced to the back door and turned the key because she had to get Marc in here. She sobbed, 'Oh, God!'

'What is it?'

'I don't know. I do know. Oh, God, I'm scared. Come with me.'

He was telling her that there was nobody in, that it was all right. But it was not all right, and she knew before she opened the living-room door that she would find him there, in what looked like a huddled heap of clothes although he was a neat and tidy dresser. Lying without sound or movement. Lying, she was dreadfully sure, without heartbeat or breath.

CHAPTER FIVE

'CALL an ambulance.' Marc's voice, sharp and urgent, reached Robin through a mist.

'He's dead.' She knew that and the horror of it paralysed her.

'Robin, *move*.' He was shouting at her now, but she couldn't move, she couldn't remember where the phone was, and then somehow she was stumbling to the little table in the hall, holding the phone in shaking fingers, trying to press 999.

When someone asked which emergency service she wanted she slmost said it was no use because he was dead. All she wanted to do was drop to the ground and howl, but she asked for 'ambulance' and she gave the address and she said, 'A heart attack.' And then she sat on the bottom of the stairs, rocking to and fro like a child.

She was useless. She had never felt as helpless before, but this was the nightmare she had always dreaded and perhaps in a little while she would be able to scream herself awake and it wouldn't have happened.

Everything was blurred. She went to the doorway but she couldn't look into the room, and then through the haze she saw that her uncle was now lying face up. Marc was kneeling beside him, mouth to mouth, and then pressing his chest. She wished she had the strength to crawl into the room and pick up her uncle's limp hand, and when Marc moved away she would, because there could be no purpose in this ritual.

She prayed wordlessly, and when she heard the sound of the siren she thought for a moment that she was screaming.

Marc said, 'That was quick.'

'What's the *use*?' she moaned.

'Open the door,' he shouted, and she went towards it like a zombie.

Men pushed past her as she turned her face to the wall, her eyes closed. She heard voices she didn't want to hear, Marc's among them, quick and concise, and after a little while the men passed her again. They were taking him away now and she stopped her ears against that and cowered at the touch of a hand on her shoulder.

'Where are they taking him?'

She thought no words had come out, but Marc said, 'To hospital. We're following.'

'But he's—' That would not come out. She could not say, Dead!

'He's in good hands. He stands a good chance.'

She couldn't believe it. It was like a miracle. Hope flared in her but she had to contain it because hysteria could hit her next. Marc was handing her the skirt that she had stripped off before climbing in the bathroom window. She managed to step into it and pull it up but she couldn't handle the zip; her fingers wouldn't move together.

He zipped it up and straightened her skirt over the waistband. Then he put his hands on her shoulders. 'Steady,' he said.

She could only nod and take strength from him. He kept an arm around her as they went out to the car.

By now a group of neighbours had gathered, realising what had happened, anxious to know more.

Marc told them in a few words as he put Robin into the passenger seat and, seeing her chalk-white face, most of them went sadly back into their homes believing that they had just seen the last of a good neighbour and a genuine gentleman.

The hospital was five miles away. The ambulance had raced ahead, with lights and sirens clearing the roads. The car went as fast as possible, but when they reached the hospital car park the stretcher had already been carried in.

Robin had never clung to anyone, but she clung to Marc Hammond now, because she was reeling and because she had no idea where to go. He got her through the doors. He sat her down while he went for information. All she could do was pray, until he came back and told her that Edward Hindley was in Emergency and the next few hours would tell them how much damage there was, how much hope.

'Can we stay?' she whispered.

'Of course.'

'Will you stay with me?'

She knew how his time was always taken up, she knew she had no claim at all, but she had known he would stay. And when he asked, 'How do we get in touch with your aunt?' she gave him the name of the woman at whose home the bridge evenings were held and left that to him as well.

Aunt Helen was next of kin; the hospital would want her contacted. Robin couldn't have spoken to her on the phone and when Marc came back and said, 'She's on her way,' Robin shuddered. 'She asked if we'd locked the house up before we left,' he went on.

'Perhaps she'll go round there to check before she comes here; I wouldn't put it past her.'

That almost made her smile but she didn't dare in case the smile went out of control, just as she hardly dared say a word. While she sat quietly she was not falling apart, and she had the crazy notion that if she went to pieces it would lessen Uncle Edward's chances of pulling through.

She would have broken down even now if Marc had not been keeping a little guard over her. From time to time nurses and men and women in white coats came along, and they talked with Marc. He seemed to know most of them and he asked questions, and the answers were encouraging, but Robin didn't think she could have done that.

Some time she would feel ashamed of herself for being so helpless, but right now she didn't feel anything but a terrible anxiety for the sick man she loved, and thankfulness for the strong man who seemed to be keeping her sane.

Aunt Helen arrived as Robin was trying to sip a cup of coffee. She marched straight up to Robin, her powdered cheeks blotched red, and demanded, 'What have you done to him?'

Robin gave a little gasp and Marc stood up, towering over Helen Hindley. 'Your niece saved your husband's life,' he said coldly. 'When there was no answer to the doorbell she got into the locked house. She called the ambulance. If he had not been found until you returned from your bridge party it would have been hours too late.'

The blotches went even brighter. Helen Hindley was taken aback. And so was Robin, who had done nothing to earn this praise. Then Helen went on another attack. 'It's worrying about you that's done this.'

Robin flinched, because there could be some truth in that poisoned barb, but Marc said, with a tigerish affability, 'Then we can reassure him that he need have no worries for Robin. She is and will continue to be well and happy.'

That was one of the last things Aunt Helen wanted to hear. A picture of frustrated spite, she stomped away and Robin whispered, 'Thank you.'

'A pleasure.' Marc sat down again, watching Helen Hindley, amused at her taking a seat as far away from them as possible. 'What a charmer,' he said. 'I hope we called her away from her first winning hand for months.' And Robin did giggle at that.

'It might have been. She doesn't often win.' She remembered and said in a sad little voice, 'Uncle Edward once said that the only thing she ever got was him and he was no prize. But he was. He *is*.'

'She could have had a prize in you too,' Marc said gently, 'if she hadn't been too stupid to see it.' He was being kind to her, she knew, but like everything about him tonight it comforted her.

The hours seemed very long. Ceaseless activity was going on but to Robin it was not real, not reaching her. She kept her eyes fixed on Marc; she listened to him. And quietly, with patience and skill, he talked her through the ordeal of waiting.

He told her what had happened to the folk she had worked with during her few days with Hammond and Hammond. Most of them were still with the firm and some of his stories—like the one about last year's Christmas party when the punch had got spiked—would have had her hooting with laughter any other time. There had been a couple of divorces, a marriage, a junior clerk graduating to senior, Edna Hodgkiss's pet poodle winning rosettes. Robin hadn't known Miss Hodgkiss had a dog, much less a county prize-winner, and although none of it was sensational news he made it all seem interesting.

She never forgot for a moment why they were here but she leaned close to him, his quiet voice reaching her and nobody else, sometimes feeling his breath on her cheek like a caress, and all the time drawing strength from his support.

Every time a doctor or a nurse came near her heart would leap. She would look towards them, then at Marc, and see from his reaction if the white-clad figure was going to stop. When she saw Marc looking towards Aunt Helen she leaned forward herself, and at the far end of the room a nurse and a man were speaking to Helen Hindley.

Robin tried to get to her feet and, as Marc stood up beside her, Aunt Helen walked away with the nurse and the man came towards them. He was smiling so it couldn't be too awful and he said, 'His wife's just gone in. She'll only stay a few minutes. He's very exhausted but comfortable and his condition, so far, is satisfactory.'

It was jargon, but it surely meant that Uncle Edward was holding his own? 'Then we can see him?' Marc asked.

'For a few seconds.'

'Of course.'

The doctor looked at Robin. 'He isn't conscious; he won't know you.'

He was warning her and she knew why. After Aunt Helen's stoicism Robin, with her wild hair and haunted eyes, looked the sort who might cause a scene. She had to swallow before she felt that her voice wouldn't let her down. Then she managed to say, 'I understand. I just want to see him breathing.'

Marc's eyes shot a quick query at the doctor and the doctor spoke to him. 'He's breathing naturally.'

'Good. We'll be here,' said Marc, and Robin sat down again, this time waiting for Aunt Helen to reappear.

Marc sat by her, silent now, and she held onto his hand. She didn't realise how hard she had been gripping until Helen Hindley came back in just over five minutes and Robin found that her fingers were numb. She hurried to her aunt but there was no softness in the older woman's face, and when Robin whispered 'How is he?' Helen Hindley's answer was almost triumphant.

'How do you expect him to be? And I'm giving instructions that you're not to see him tonight.'

Robin had no fight in her. She would have accepted that with only a choked protest but Marc said, 'As a lawyer, madam, I would not advise that.'

He spoke quietly, but Marc Hammond could always give out danger signals and Robin saw her aunt's expression change from malice to apprehension. Helen Hindley was not tangling with Marc Hammond. She huffed and puffed and marched away and Robin asked Marc, 'Can she stop me seeing him?'

'Possibly. Temporarily. But she won't.' He grinned and she thought, You have the nicest smile of anyone I've ever known. 'She's scared we might sue her,' he said cheerfully, and she thought how she would love to set Marc Hammond on her aunt, because she had never seen anyone scare Helen before.

Edward Hindley lay in a narrow bed in a little room and Robin kept her gaze on his face. He was pale but he always was pale, and he looked as if he was sleeping peacefully. She tried to block out the equipment, that screen where the heartbeats made a regular pattern and which she had seen in countless TV hospital dramas when an alarm rang and the line went flat and unbroken and deadly.

She said softly, 'It's Robin. You're going to be fine. Rest now; I'll be back tomorrow. I love you so very much.' And she thought he nearly smiled but that could have been wishful thinking.

In the car Marc asked her, 'All right?'

She said, 'Yes, thank you,' and for the rest of the journey she went on praying.

Elsie and Maybelle were waiting. Marc had rung them earlier from the hospital and now he told them, and Robin knew that this was to reassure her too, that Edward Hindley was recovering. Maybelle had been worried about Robin and even Elsie seemed concerned, although Robin insisted that she was fine. She was tired, of course—it was past midnight—and bed was where she should be, said Maybelle.

Elsie made her a hot milk drink and the three women went upstairs to their rooms. On the landing Maybelle kissed Robin's cheek and said, 'Goodnight, my dear.'

Elsie said, 'You get some rest now.'

Robin smiled at them and went into her room. She put the hot milk down very carefully on her dressing table. In the shower room she stripped off, splashing her face and hands with cold water, pulling a nightshirt over her head. It was a warm night, but her skin felt clammy and goose-pimply inside the cool cotton, and before she could reach the bed her eyes filled with tears. They ran down her cheeks and a storm of weeping swept over her as she fell in a huddle on the bed, shoulders hunched and head bowed, and it was as if she were weeping the tears of a lifetime.

When the knock came on the door she tried to gasp, Go away, but the door opened and Marc came in.

'How are you?' he said. 'And that's a damn fool question when I know how you are.'

Did he mean he had realised how she was feeling when she hadn't known herself that she had reached breaking-point? She could hardly see him for tears, and when he sat on the bed beside her she went into his arms without a word.

She had never had a man holding her while she sobbed before—not a father, a brother, a friend or a lover. Perhaps her mother had when she was a baby, but she couldn't remember that. There had been no one since, and in Marc Hammond's arms tonight she was almost as weak as a child. But she knew he would hold her for hours if need be, because he was the one in all the world who could make her strong again.

When the tears ran out her throat was raw and aching as she choked, 'I'm sorry; I was no help at all. I did nothing. If I'd been on my own I couldn't have done anything.'

He rocked and comforted her, telling her what she needed to hear. 'It's all right; it's all right.'

With her wet cheek against the damp shoulder of his jacket she took a gulp of air and stammered, 'H-he's always had this heart thing. He had rheumatic fever when he was very young and he's had attacks before but never as bad as this. And I've always been scared,

right from my schooldays, of coming into the house
and finding him just like he was lying then. And really
being alone because he is the only one who has ever
really loved me.'

He let her go on talking, telling him how good a
man her uncle was, how kind, of the quiet ways in
which he had made her life bearable when Aunt Helen
had been throwing her weight about. This might not
have impressed Marc, who wouldn't have much sympathy for a man who let a bossy woman tyrannise him,
but he let her talk.

'I couldn't have saved him,' she said at last.

'You would have done.'

It had been a very close thing—a few minutes could
have made a terrible difference, and for those first
minutes Robin had been deranged with shock and
grief. She said, facing facts, 'I don't think so, but you
did and I'll never be able to thank you enough.'

'You already have,' he said, and he was used to
taking charge so perhaps it hadn't seemed all that
much to him, but she would never forget what a rock
he had been, there and at the hospital.

'You got me in to see him too,' she said. 'Aunt
Helen could have stopped me tonight. Anybody could
have stopped me tonight.'

'They won't tomorrow,' he said. Her eyelids were
pink and puffy and in the light from a single lamp she
wasn't seeing too clearly, but she could see his face
bending over her, and the start of a smile that lifted
the corner of his mouth.

'No, tomorrow I'll be a toughie again.' She made
her own lips curve. 'I hope.' She would have liked to
feel his mouth on hers, just brushing, to see how it felt,
how it tasted. A kiss between friends. A goodnight

kiss. She had had plenty of those, plenty of lovers' kisses too, but her tongue flickered over her lips, which were suddenly hot and swollen, and she moved back a little. 'What must I look like?' That was nearly a joke. She had to look a fright.

'Does it matter?'

Of course it didn't matter to him what she looked like, but she liked the way *he* looked. That was because he had come to her rescue, so that everything that was dangerous and threatening in him had been working for her not against her. She was looking at him without prejudice, with gratitude, and he looked hard and handsome and stunningly sexy.

Her puffy eyes must have opened wide, because that shook her, and made her realise how light-headed she was, to get a mind-blowing jolt of lust like that. She began to dab her cheeks with her fingertips, although she had rubbed most of the wetness into his jacket, and he took out a white handkerchief and handed it to her.

She would have liked him to do the drying, patting under her eyes, smoothing across her cheekbones down to her jawline. She would have liked him to touch her tenderly after the comfort of hugging, and when he lifted a hank of heavy hair from her forehead it was like an electric shock, nearly strong enough to make her hair stand on end.

She began jittering, pushing back her hair herself, laughing on a wobbly note, assuring him, 'I'm not hysterical,' although she wasn't sure about that. 'But I was praying all the time tonight, promising anything— you know, how children do.'

He smiled at her but his eyes were in darkness, and she wondered if he had ever prayed childish prayers,

and if the last time might have been when they'd
brought news of a burned-out car in the Welsh moun-
tains. Please, God, don't let it be them. . .

She had to make him really smile, and she said gaily,
'I promised I'd cut off my hair if he pulled through,
although I don't know what good I thought that would
do.'

Then the gleam of amusement was in his eyes too. 'I
should wait for your uncle's opinion on that. I don't
think he'd be for cutting your hair.'

'Aunt Helen would.' She pulled a face. 'She went
spare when I wouldn't have it plaited any more. The
first time I brushed it loose and shook it all about I felt
wonderfully wild and wicked.'

She tossed her hair back now and he laughed. 'And
you have been ever since.'

'You think so?'

'Wonderfully,' he said.

Any minute he would get up and leave her. The
weeping jag was over and he had already spent hours
holding her hand through tonight's ordeal. But she
wanted him to stay longer, talking to her, making her
smile. She would like to lie here all night, with his arm
around her, breathing in the clean male smell of him.

She began to tell him about Uncle Edward teaching
her to drive and how they had used to creep out, going
miles away before she took the wheel, hoping no one
would spot them. It made a funny tale, Robin hiding
her hair under a scarf and Aunt Helen demanding,
when she'd passed her test, 'Which of your fancy men
gave you lessons?'

Then the phone rang and all the warmth went out of
her. Marc jumped up and she knew it was the hospital
and that a phone call this late could only mean one

thing. 'Stay here,' he ordered from the bedroom door, but she was right behind him, and this time there was not even time to start praying.

There was a phone extension in Maybelle's sitting room, and there was probably another in his bedroom, but he hurried downstairs to the one in the hall and Robin nearly fell after him. If she hadn't grabbed the handrail she would have pitched down. She stood at the bottom of the stairs as he said, 'Hammond here.' Then he saw her and gave a resigned shrug, enough to reassure her it was not the hospital.

The relief made her sag back against the wall. 'Leave it to me,' said Marc after listening briefly, and he hung up. 'An idiot getting himself breathalysed in a speed trap,' he told her. 'Phoning from the police station.'

'He wants you there?' She couldn't hide the wistfulness in her voice; if the phone rang again how could she handle it if he was not here?

'Dominic, I think.' He might have delegated in any case. Caught in a speed check the driver was unlikely to have done anything worse than speeding. A 'guilty' plea would be a foregone conclusion; he wouldn't need the big legal gun to deal with that.

She said, 'Please send Dominic.'

'Go back to bed.' He was tapping a number and sounded like a father with a child who should have been asleep hours ago.

'Will you look in? Just to say goodnight?' He nodded before he spoke.

'Sorry about this, Lucy; would you put Dom on?'

She hadn't remembered that she was in such a skimpy shirt, and that under it were bare legs, bare everything. She went quickly up the stairs and she supposed she might look as he probably saw her—as

hardly more than a child. At the top of the stairs she
glanced down again; he was still on the phone, and she
thought, I am not that young.

But she was young enough for near-nakedness to
make her self-conscious, and she left her door open,
turned off the bedside lamp, and climbed into bed with
the sheets held high enough to cover all but her
shoulders. Warm again now, she felt the blood coursing
through her veins, bringing a flush to her cheeks and
making her whole body glow.

Almost at once Marc appeared in the doorway.
Light from the landing behind him made him appear
taller than ever and Robin held her breath. 'Goodnight,' he said.

'Oh! Goodnight!'

'Try not to worry; he is going to pull through.'

'I know.' She was confident of that now and so
thankful.

He closed the door and a few moments later she saw
the thread of light around her door go out, leaving the
landing in darkness.

She could not have been happier about her uncle,
but at the same time she was aware of a crushing
disappointment because Marc had closed the door and
gone. She had wanted him to come back—not just to
say goodnight, nor to put a friendly arm around her
and talk of everyday things, but to touch her and kiss
her passionately and make sweet and savage love to
her. Because in the past few hours Robin had found
the man who could set her on fire. It was a chemistry
she had never experienced or believed in before, but
perhaps she had had warning over the years.

She lay back in the darkness, remembering how her
breath had caught when she'd first seen him three

years ago, and since then, watching for him, knowing he would be there, getting the vibes when she saw him in town and hurrying away in panic. From what? Nothing, her mind and reason were telling her, but her nerves and her instinct, her blood and her bones could have got the message that he was her fate.

That was crazy. That was going right over the top. But if he had come into her room before he'd closed the door, and come to her bed, she would have slipped out of the silly nightshirt and helped him slip off his jacket, tear off his shirt. She would have touched his skin with her skin, done anything he wanted because he could be everything she wanted and she pressed her face into the pillow and moaned softly, biting her lower lip until the pain of that reached her.

She might have drawn blood. She rolled over, the back of her hand against her mouth, and tried to tell herself that she was out of her mind tonight. She was churned up in every way; tomorrow she would be a toughie again. And she had to be bone-weary, but she couldn't get to sleep until she imagined that Marc was lying beside her, stroking her hair. Then she relaxed, breathing deeply, her limbs as heavy and languid as if they had just made love. . .

It was daylight when she woke, just after seven, and she remembered how ill her uncle was. But there had been no calls so he had made it through the night, and this morning she was more hopeful that he would pull through.

She remembered Marc and wondered if she had dreamed about him while she'd slept, but between closing her eyes and pretending he was lying beside her there seemed to have been only the quiet dark.

Last night had been frantic. She had never felt desire like that before—a raging hunger as if she would starve to death without him.

She could have followed him when he'd walked away, gone nearly naked to his room, and that would have been crazy. She was so glad she had not done that. In the cold light of day she knew it would have made her look pathetic because, of course, he would have sent her back to her own bed.

Marc's handkerchief was on the pillow beside her, where she had dropped it after wiping away the tear marks. She picked it up and put it against her cheek again, and realised ruefully that daylight wasn't making much difference—she still fancied him madly. And it couldn't be reaction to stress and fear this morning, when she was alight with excitement just at the thought that she would be seeing him again in no time at all. He usually left the house early and she had to get downstairs before he went.

She flung back the bedclothes and dashed into the shower room. When she came out she started scrambling into clothes, then saw last night's untouched milk drink on the dressing table, revolting with a wrinkled skin on top, and poured that away. Just in time, because there was a tap on the door, followed immediately by Elsie with a cup of tea.

This morning Elsie's smile was friendly. 'Ah,' she said, 'You're up. I was going to tell you he had a comfortable night; Marc rang the hospital.'

'Thank you,' said Robin.

'There's no rush,' said Elsie. 'Maybelle's not awake yet. You drink your tea and come down when you're ready.'

Robin could have run down as she was, half-dressed,

to catch Marc, because it seemed that if she didn't see him and speak to him before he left the day would be off to a bad start. But Marc and Elsie would think she was dotty if she did that, and she finished dressing fast.

Her tangled hair brought tears to her eyes when she tried to tug a comb through it, so she brushed it quickly into some sort of order instead. Her skin needed little make-up, but she thought she was pale, and pinched her cheeks and looked at herself in the mirror. He had said she was beautiful—looking like a top model, he had said. But so were other girls; she wasn't going to dazzle him.

It was more than likely that she wasn't his type at all. Going by Leila she certainly wasn't. Leila was cool and cutting and classy, and Robin was trouble, and although he could handle trouble that didn't mean he wanted it around. So far all Robin had proved was her nuisance value, and when he saw her this morning he might be untouchable again.

She gulped some of the scalding tea and poured the rest of that away too, then went downstairs with her heart in her throat. Well, that was how it felt, because it was there that a pulse was throbbing away, and as she reached the bottom of the stairs he came out of the study.

She stopped suddenly, the empty teacup she was holding rattling on the saucer. He reached her in a couple of strides, took the cup and saucer and put them down on an oak chest in the hall. He didn't put his arms around her, just his hands on her shoulders, but that was a kind of bonding, and they looked at each other in silence for a few seconds.

'How are you?' he asked.

'Good,' she said. 'Really good this morning.'

'That's my girl.' She knew it was just a saying, but this time surely it had to mean more?

Elsie came from the kitchen and said, 'Now you're down you can take Maybelle's tea up.'

'You can see him this morning,' Marc said. 'I'm off to the office now; I'll see you there, say, one o'clock?'

Robin nodded, eyes dancing because of the way Marc was smiling—as if he might have kissed her if Elsie had not walked into the hall.

Robin was not fooling herself that he felt the same as she did. He was not crazy for her, but last night had started something between them. She was not over-confident—she was not really confident at all—but now it seemed as if there had never been any other man in her past, that she had always been waiting for Marc and he was the lover for the rest of her life.

It hurt her to leave him. She had to take the cup of tea from Elsie when she wanted to go to his car with him, and say, Goodbye for now, and watch him drive away as if she was the woman he would be coming home to.

So she was, in a way, but now she went quietly into the bedroom where Maybelle was already awake, sitting up and asking 'How is he?' Maybelle Myson had never met Uncle Edward, but she was anxious about him and Robin loved her for that.

She said, 'Marc rang the hospital. He had a good night. I can see him this morning. Will that be all right?'

Of course it would. Maybelle was lunching with a friend and Robin could drop her off at the friend's house any time after breakfast, collecting her when-ever it was convenient.

'Marc said to go into the office about one o'clock,' said Robin.

'He'll want to know how your uncle is,' Maybelle said.

Yes, although he could always find that out by picking up a phone. Robin was almost sure he wanted to see her, and she said, 'My uncle was unconscious when we found him and I went into shock. Marc kept him breathing.'

That didn't surprise Maybelle. She sipped her tea, her clear eyes on Robin. 'There's nobody like Marc in an emergency.'

'He was wonderful,' breathed Robin.

'He often is,' Maybelle said drily. 'That could be why women make fools of themselves over him.'

Maybelle was warning her, so she must be looking starry-eyed. Robin had told Maybelle Myson things she had told nobody else. She was the wise old grandmother Robin needed, but no way could Robin tell her now, I don't care if I do make a fool of myself, because I know that Marc is the man for me, and if I am ever going to reach the stars Marc will have to be with me.

She wished she could ask, How did you know that the man you married was the only one for you? Even death had not dimmed Maybelle's love affair. But for now Robin must hide her feelings, because they were only making Maybelle anxious.

One way to hide them was not to talk about Marc, to resist the temptation to say even his name. Robin liked the sound of it so much that she wanted to go on repeating, Marc, Marc, Marc, like a song. She would have liked to ask Maybelle a hundred things about him but she didn't.

They sat over breakfast, with the newspapers and Maybelle's mail, and then Robin took the wheel and drove Maybelle to her friend's home, which was a pretty bungalow in a pretty garden. She stopped on the way to the hospital, to buy flowers and grapes and a paperback thriller that looked an easy read and although her uncle, in Intensive Care, didn't seem up to reading anything yet, he smiled when he saw her and they joked about the pink carnations.

There was no one else by his bed. Robin drew up a chair and beamed at him. 'I don't know what your favourite flowers are; I've never bought you flowers before.'

'I don't think I've got a favourite flower,' he said, 'but from now on I'm a pink-carnation man.'

She talked quietly to him, telling him about Maybelle Myson, the house, the work she did. 'Was Marc Hammond here last night?' Edward Hindley asked.

'Yes.' She wondered what vague images had moved through his unconsciousness.

'Are you happy, Robin?' Her uncle still thought she was living with Marc, and in her heart she was, in every way.

Now she smiled and said, 'Very happy this morning, but last night I was in a right state.'

'So was I,' said Uncle Edward, and they were both smiling when Aunt Helen walked in, carrying a pot plant and a bag that probably contained more grapes. She gave the man on the bed a quick, summing-up glance then turned on Robin.

'I hope you haven't been overtiring him.'

'Not me,' said Robin gaily. 'But as soon as they unhitch him from this lot we're going disco dancing.'

She got up from the chair, on which Aunt Helen promptly plonked herself, and bent over to kiss her uncle's cheek and whisper, 'I'll be back.'

He was getting better. He would need nursing, careful watching, but he wanted to get well, he would do as he was told. This morning everything seemed possible to Robin. She drove out of the hospital car park into the sunshine, parked not far from the river, and walked along the tow-path, killing time until she was due to meet Marc.

This wasn't a date as such but her spirits were so buoyant that she could have been dancing on air. She smiled at strangers who looked at her, as strangers often did, and moved on, her long legs carrying her swiftly away before they were sure she had smiled.

At ten minutes to one she turned Mrs Myson's car through the archway that was part of the Georgian building that was Hammond and Hammond's in the town square, and into the first vacant car space. Marc's Mercedes was in the reserved space his car had occupied when Robin had worked here, and she wondered which was Dominic's car, if he was in the office. She would have guessed his to be a rakish sports number because, as Mrs Myson said, Dominic was still a schoolboy at heart.

The foyer hadn't changed since Robin had left it in disgrace—marbled tiles on the floor, panelled walls, a few expensive-looking leather armchairs, a large floral display in an alcove and two women behind the reception counter. One Robin didn't know, but she looked efficient and suitable. The other was Miss Hodgkiss, who was three years older and hadn't changed her hairstyle from a neat bob, nor her dress style—she was still in a darkish suit and a crisp white blouse.

The way she looked at Robin was much the same too. For the few days they had worked together Edna Hodgkiss had continuously been uneasy because her assistant had seemed so out of place. After the fight she had been slack-jawed with horror, but now it was the guarded look that Robin was getting.

'Mr Hammond is expecting you,' Miss Hodgkiss said as Robin walked towards the counter. 'If you'd take a seat I'll let him know you're here.'

Robin sat down and a couple of minutes later Dominic came running down the stairs, calling, 'Robin!' as he came, so that Robin wondered briefly if the wrong Hammond had got the message. But this meeting was accidental and a delight to Dominic, who almost hauled her to her feet. 'You're a sight for sore eyes,' he said. Then he stopped grinning. 'Sorry about your uncle; that must have been nasty for you, but he's doing all right, isn't he?'

'He's doing fine,' said Robin, and it was lovely to know it was true.

Her glow of happiness lit up her face and her eyes and Dominic asked lightly, 'How come you've got even prettier? Are you in love?'

That was true too, although he was joking, and Robin gave a little spurt of laughter. 'Not me,' she said.

'Anyway,' said Dominic, 'you look good enough to eat.'

She was aware of several folk in the foyer watching them, and how flirtatious this exchange might seem, and she said, 'Don't try it.'

'As if I would. Reporting to Marc, are you?'

'That's right.'

'We all do, and here he is.'

Marc was coming down the stairs and Dominic stepped back quickly as if he had been standing too close to Robin, and she didn't even see him go because when Marc was near Dominic became almost invisible. Like everyone else in the foyer, in the street, in the world, he faded into a hazy background.

Marc didn't grab Robin as Dominic had but he might as well have done, because when he smiled and said, 'Hello,' and looked into her eyes it seemed like a deep kiss, stopping her breath so that she couldn't say a word.

Walking out of the building, he put a hand under her elbow and asked, 'You've seen him?' If it had been bad news she would have been drawing strength from him again. If she had stumbled he would have supported her. She said, 'He's doing fine, cracking little jokes. We were both grinning away when Aunt Helen arrived, with a bag of something and a pot plant.'

'A cactus?'

She giggled. 'It should have been but it had green leaves and buds, and she'll be taking it back when he goes home again. Where are we going?'

They were crossing the square and it didn't matter where they were going because she would happily have gone anywhere. 'Let's eat,' he said.

Little cul-de-sacs and small shopping precincts ran off the square, and in the summer season there were plenty of cafés, all cheerful and inviting. Several had tables set out on the pavement and they took a table under a striped blue and white awning.

The speciality here was Greek food, and Robin had village salad, with tomatoes, cucumber, onions, olives and feta cheese. Marc had a seafood platter, and in the sunshine under a bright blue sky, with diners and strollers in summery clothes, most of them holiday-makers, Robin felt that they could have been on one of the Greek islands.

She had taken self-catering breaks abroad with friends, and had sipped frosted drinks as she was now, and, although Marc was wearing a lightweight but very formal suit, shirt and tie, she could imagine him in an open-necked shirt, sipping ouzo, and afterwards taking her back to a villa for two, or perhaps to a boat for sailing off to another island.

Several passers-by recognised Robin. Most of the young ones called, 'Hi,' and one young man stopped in his tracks to gasp, '*Robin*!'

'Hello,' she said sweetly. 'This is—'

'I know who it is.' He was recognising Marc Hammond. 'What have you been up to?'

'You'd be surprised,' said Robin.

'No, I wouldn't,' he muttered, backing away. He never felt comfortable near men who could wipe the floor with him, and he had always thought Robin Johnson was a wild one.

'You would,' she said softly to his vanishing figure, and Marc laughed. 'He thought you were my lawyer,' she explained.

'That he did.'

'As if I could afford you.'

'Oh, I don't know,' said Marc. 'I come reasonable for deserving cases.'

'I'll make a note of it.'

They talked in the sunshine and she answered every question he asked, easily and naturally. She told him all she knew about her parents. Her father had been an American student and had gone back home before Jenny, her mother, had known for sure that she was pregnant. She hadn't written to tell him. She'd had friends, and had obviously been a happy-go-lucky girl, younger than Robin herself was now when Robin had been born. Five years later, while they were living in a commune in Cornwall, Jenny had caught flu, and had succumbed to one of those swift killer viruses that strike about one in a thousand.

'Uncle Edward and Aunt Helen fetched me,' Robin told Marc, 'and I've lived with them ever since. She was always saying she hoped she knew her duty, and I was fed and housed, kept clean and tidy, but it was my uncle who wanted me with them.'

'Will she look after him?' Marc asked. 'He'll need nursing.'

'Oh, she'll do her duty, and whether she likes it or not I won't be far away; I'll see that he's all right.'

'Would she agree to a nurse living in?'

'I don't think they could afford it.'

'That's no problem,' he said, and professional nursing for her uncle would have been a tremendous relief to Robin, but she couldn't expect Marc to finance it.

Aunt Helen wouldn't turn down discreet aid that meant she could swank to her friends about a live-in nurse, but it might worry Uncle Edward. He was a proud man. And Robin must not impose too much on Marc's support.

Elbows on the table, chin on her linked fingers, she looked thoughtful. 'I'd like him to have a nurse, of course,' she said. 'Tender loving care has never been Aunt Helen's style, but I'd want to pay towards the costs.'

'Fair enough. I'll send you an account.' He smiled at

her, and they could have been talking legal terms but they were not.

They were friends. And lovers on a Greek island, Robin thought, enjoying her fantasy. Beneath the well-cut jacket she could imagine the broad shoulders and the ripple of muscles over the ribcage. On a Greek island she would have run raking fingers down his chest. Undressing with the eyes was supposed to be a male prerogative and she wondered if he saw her shoulders gleaming naked under the thin shirt that covered them.

Perhaps he did because his smile had more than a hint of devilment. And she laughed with a flash of perfect teeth and a toss of her red hair as almost every local passing by turned to stare, at Robin Johnson and the very eligible, very dangerous Marc Hammond smiling at each other across the café table.

CHAPTER SIX

MARC and Robin walked back together to where she had left Maybelle's car in the car park behind the offices. For Robin this was surely the loveliest day of the year. All the colours were dazzling, and voices and footsteps, even the traffic, were like the sounds of music.

In the car park heads turned, as clients and staff tried to work out whether the redhead with Marc Hammond was a friend or a client. In the driving seat of the car she wound down the window and said, 'Thanks for lunch,' and again his smile seemed to touch her lips with swift, sensuous pressure.

At the archway into the square she looked back and he was still standing there, and she blew him a mischievous kiss which ought to have been a clue, for the ones who were still staring, that Marc Hammond and the redhead were very close friends at least.

It was just after two o'clock—time to check when Maybelle wanted taking home. She was sitting on the patio behind the bungalow, with one of the friends Robin had met on Monday evening. The woman of the house Robin didn't know, but she was the same age as Maybelle and looked like Maybelle's friend. Maybelle Myson herself had the special spark and spirit that meant she would have been the rebel of the gang since schooldays.

The remains of a salad lunch were on the table, with

three glasses and a nearly empty bottle of white wine, and Maybelle was ready to go home.

She kissed both her friends on the cheek and told them to be good. 'We'll be round for you about half-nine on Wednesday,' she told her hostess, and Robin wondered if she shoud be helping her into the car—until Maybelle nipped in unaided. The wine didn't seem to have affected her balance at all.

'How was your uncle?' she asked.

'In Intensive Care, of course,' said Robin, 'but he is going to be all right, though he's still very groggy.'

'You won't want to be leaving him, then?'

'*Leaving* him?'

'Betty and I are going to Bournemouth for a few days from Wednesday. You could have come with us but I suppose you should be staying here.'

Yes, she should. She had to be around. Nor did she want to leave Marc. She said, 'I must go in each day.'

'Of course you must,' said Maybelle. 'And there's plenty you can do. Marc's bringing a typewriter for me; there are all sorts of papers that would be better typed. You've seen Marc?'

'Yes. We had lunch.'

'I'm surprised he could spare the time,' said Maybelle, and to stop her asking questions Robin began to chatter about the weather being just right for taking a break at the seaside.

At six o'clock she was back at the hospital. She had left Maybelle having her siesta, done some shopping for her, and was checking on her uncle again before she returned to the house. He was looking tired still but his eyes brightened when Robin reached the side of his bed. 'No pink carnations this time,' she said.

'Just me for five minutes then I have to get back on duty.'

He said, 'It's good to see you.' She thought that of course she couldn't go away until he was out of danger. She sat beside him and asked, 'Is there anything you want, anything I can bring you?'

'No, I've got everything I need.' He had something else on his mind. 'What happened? I was waiting for you and Marc Hammond. Did you find me?'

She said, 'Marc did everything. According to the book, I guess. I'm so grateful to him.'

'Your aunt told me you were living with him.'

'I'm working for his aunt, Mrs Myson—I told you about her.'

'Well,' said Edward Hindley, 'I'm grateful to him but I don't want you feeling in his debt.' Robin's lips curved.

'Goodness, no,' she said. 'I'm just glad he was there.'

Some time she would tell Uncle Edward how glad she was that Marc was with her. But not just yet. If she had said, I'm not only grateful to him but after last night I've suddenly found I'm crazy about him, that would have sent her uncle's temperature soaring.

Driving back to the house, she had that feeling of coming home again, and of course it wasn't just the house. Nor only Maybelle. It was because this was Marc's home and the thought of getting back to him filled her with contentment.

As she was waiting, signalling right, for a break in the main-road traffic so that she could turn into the drive, another car was coming out. Robin took a quick look at the girl at the wheel—very pretty with short, bouncy honey-blonde hair—and got a fleeting stare back. Then the sports car was gone and Robin turned in.

Marc's car was in the garage and that made her smile, and when she went into the kitchen Elsie said, 'She's in the drawing room; did you get her stuff?' Robin had had a list, ranging from a special handcream to a pair of very lightweight support hose.

'It's all here.' Robin waved the shopping bag.

In the drawing room Maybelle was sitting in an armchair, Marc was standing, and Robin wondered if he had just come into the room after saying goodbye to the girl in the car. And she wondered who she was.

Maybelle answered that, saying regretfully, 'You've just missed Lucy. You'll like her; she's a dear girl.'

'Dominic's girl,' said Marc.

'They're getting married in October,' said Maybelle, as if she didn't approve of this living-together lifestyle. Robin doubted if a wedding would stop Dominic flirting, although his womanising might be all talk, but Lucy was pretty, and if Maybelle thought she was a dear girl she probably was. 'That's nice,' said Robin, and hoped they would be happy.

'So what are you doing with the rest of the evening?' Marc enquired.

'Me?' He was looking at Robin so he had to mean her. 'Nothing,' she said, and looked at Maybelle.

'Then I'll take you out to dinner,' said Marc, and she kept looking at Maybelle, who might be finding something for her to do. But Maybelle sat quietly, although her expression could have been disapproving, and Marc laughed. 'Do you know why she's always wanted a granddaughter?' he asked Robin. 'So that she could warn her against the wicked ways of men like me.'

'What nonsense you talk,' Maybelle protested, and Robin lowered her lashes to veil her shining eyes.

'Ready in half an hour?' he said.

'I could be, yes,' she said calmly. 'And I would like to go out to dinner.'

'Like' was not the right word when it was something she was absolutely thrilled about, but she handed over the shopping and went sedately upstairs. And as soon as she closed the door of her room she kicked off her shoes and whirled round and round in a dance of sheer glee. Ready in half an hour? She could have been ready in five minutes. She could have moved at the speed of light if necessary, so that thirty minutes seemed a leisurely preparation.

She was in the shower and out of it. She had pushed her hair into a shower cap to keep it dry and now it fell over her shoulders, reaching her waist in a burnished cloud.

She put on the bracelet that Maybelle had given her, and the copper-coloured dress she had bought on her first day out with Maybelle, and regarded herself anxiously in the mirror.

She was a looker—she would have been blind if she couldn't see that—but deep down there was an insecurity that Helen Hindley had kept alive. Robin attracted men, with no trouble at all, because she looked the way she did, but it had never mattered much before. Tonight, when she desperately wanted to be sexy and smart, she wasn't sure she could be either.

Maybelle was alone in the drawing room now, and when Robin walked in she said, 'You look pretty.'

'Thank you.' Robin had been going to ask, You don't think I should fasten my hair back, and this dress is all right, isn't it? because she needed reassuring, but

Maybelle said, 'Marc's in the study. Run along now and have your dinner.' And Robin went, nervously smoothing down her hair, breathing deeply for a few seconds before she tapped on the closed door.

This was only having a meal together, for heaven's sake. It was hardly a commitment when a man said casually, If you're doing nothing this evening we'll go out to dinner. But she suddenly felt gauche and shy, and awkward enough to trip over her own feet.

Marc opened the door, dark-suited, clean-shaven, immaculate, and she didn't have to ask, Will I do? because the admiration in his smile was unmistakable. She was the one he wanted to be with this evening, and her confidence came bounding back.

As the car drew out of the drive he asked, 'Did Maybelle tell you to be home by midnight?'

'No. Why?'

He laughed. 'She's chaperoning you. It's the grandmother complex. I never knew she wanted a granddaughter until you told me.'

'And she thinks I need protection from you?' she said that lightly and he was still smiling.

'Which we both know you do not. But if you did the path of seduction would not run smoothly while Maybelle had her eyes on us.'

'Oh, I believe that,' said Robin, and she did, but in a few days Maybelle was off on holiday. Elsie would turn a blind eye. Robin would almost be alone with Marc. She looked out of the window, because the car had slowed for the roundabout and she didn't want him looking into her face and reading her thoughts.

They bypassed the town centre, cutting through the countryside to another town. On the way music played on the radio, and there was nothing of the austere

Marc Hammond in this amusing, sexy man who was her companion tonight.

The Royal Hotel was the oldest and plushest in this town, and the Actors' Bar was the most expensive and exclusive of its three restaurants. Actors had used it when the old music hall had stood opposite. That site had been a shopping precinct for years but the hotel had prospered. The name of the Actors' Bar remained, although, with a famous chef in the kitchen, starched linen tablecloths and silver service, prices had soared since the day of the jobbing actors.

The decor was still Victorian—red and gold wallpaper, red plush seats, and chandeliers glittering overhead. On summer evenings a pianist played and tables edged a space for dancing, and it was fun and a treat for Robin. 'This is gorgeous,' she said as they were seated at a table just far enough from the pianist, almost in privacy. Most of the other tables were filled and she asked, 'Do you come here often?'

'No,' he said, 'but the food's good. We got a cancellation.'

'I bet you always do.'

And she laughed when he said, 'I've a pretty good average.'

They consulted the menu and ordered, and she looked up at the crystals of the chandelier overhead. They were as dazzling as diamonds and she was already having a brilliant time. The food tasted as good as it looked, and Marc kept her smiling and she felt pretty and witty, swapping stories with him, coming out with quips.

The pianist had been playing all through their meal, couples had been dancing, and she asked, 'Do you dance?'

'I can move around but I might come heavy on your feet.'

'I'll chance it.' She stood up and moved into his arms. The music was dreamy and she melted against him in a sensation of pure joy. This was what she wanted—moving to the beat, eyes closed, with his arms around her, his mouth so close that he could have bowed his head and kissed her.

Then he trod on her toes, and she yelped and hopped before she could help it, and the dancers around them smiled. 'I'm sorry,' he said, 'but I did warn you.'

'How come you're so light on your feet and so heavy on mine?'

'One of life's mysteries.'

'It's nice to know even Marc Hammond isn't an expert on everything,' she teased.

'Everything? I could make a very long list of failures for you.'

'I'd love to see that but you won't write it.'

'No, I won't. Shall we give this up?'

'You're not getting out of it that easily,' she said. 'You stand, I'll dance.'

That was how most of them were dancing—circling each other, swaying, jigging. Robin danced with Marc, usually at arm's length, but touching hands to shoulders, reaching for him and laughing because he was smiling at her. And it was the most sensual dancing that she had ever known, because although they were apart the electricity between them was so strong that she felt it in every nerve.

When the pianist finished the medley and reached for a long cool lager, Robin felt as if this had been nearer to lovemaking than respectable dancing in a public place. It was Marc, of course, the way he turned her on just being near her, and she had to behave and be sensible or she could lose her head completely.

Time went all too quickly. They were home well before twelve, but the windows of Maybelle's room were dark and Elsie had gone to bed. As he'd driven back Robin had still been lit up from the lights and the music and the heady delight of Marc Hammond's constant and undivided attention.

Half the time she'd hardly known what she was saying as she'd babbled happily, about the other diners—she had recognised several—about the food, going over the tunes again, singing a few lines of one song in her husky, slightly off-key voice.

When he'd smiled at that she'd laughed, 'I never could sing in tune. At singsongs I'm always the one miming.'

When they came into the silent house she said, 'I had a lovely time.'

'So did I.'

'And Cinderella's back before midnight.'

'That should please the fairy godmother,' he said.

She didn't want the evening to end with her going to her room alone. She had never had to make the advances before. Holding off men had been her problem. Marc was the most sophisticated man she had ever come up against and if he had further plans for tonight he would move in with practised ease. But he was saying goodnight to her at the foot of the stairs and she had to be the one to ask, 'Will you walk with me in the garden?' He had to know she meant, Come out with me under the moon and make love to me.

'Not tonight,' he said, but it was a refusal without a sting because he spoke so gently that it was a promise.

'Some other evening?' she said.

'Some other evening,' he promised.

He would have kissed her she was almost sure, but she said, 'I'll see you tomorrow,' and ran quickly up the stairs. If he had kissed her she would have clung to him; she wouldn't have been able to help it. And he was right. Tonight was too soon.

He found her attractive, he thought she was special, and nothing would be lost by waiting a little longer. Going too fast could mean missing something. He had a cool head, and she trusted his judgement.

It astounded her how completely she was trusting him. Her desire for him had surprised her too—she had never experienced this passionate longing before. But she realised now that it was as if she had known him all her life and he had never let her down.

He could have been the one she'd turned to when Aunt Helen had been rubbishing her. Uncle Edward had tried to encourage her but if Marc Hammond had said, You're a bright girl, she would have believed him. She would have taken his advice. Maybe she was born to be wild but she would have listened to him if he had been her friend. He was her friend now. And he would be her lover. So whatever the future brought she would always have him to rely on. That was taking a lot for granted, but she fell asleep smiling, and when she woke she still believed it.

Maybelle and her friend were off on Wednesday. Robin was driving them down to the small hotel in Bournemouth that they had used for years, then bringing herself back here the same day. She would drive down again to collect them early the week after next, unless they decided they were enjoying themselves enough to stay a few days longer.

Meanwhile Robin was busy ferrying Maybelle here and there, from her friends, her hairdresser and her chiropodist, to pick up boxes and bags containing clothes, bric-a-brac and books that were being donated for various charities.

Robin saw Marc most mornings and every evening. Only for a few minutes in the mornings because he always left early. But it only took a few minutes to exchange a look, a word that told her what she needed to know, that he was on her side, that if she needed him he would be here for her.

Most evenings he worked late, sometimes out, sometimes in his study, but he always looked for Robin when he came in, as if he was more than pleased to see her. And her heart would beat, fierce and fast, with a surge of passion and longing.

During the day, if she could manage it, and always in the evenings, she called into the hospital, where Uncle Edward was looking better and getting stronger. There was an impressive show of flowers, plants and get-well cards around his bed, and he was surprised and touched that so many people were remembering him.

Robin was not surprised—he was a lovely man—and when she bumped into Aunt Helen on one of her visits she said, 'Isn't he popular?' and told Marc that evening, 'She looked as if she thought they'd all been delivered to the wrong bed.'

When she told Maybelle how many visitors he was getting, and how he was improving, Maybelle said, 'I suppose you wouldn't like to stay with Betty and me after all?' and Robin went panicky, babbling,

'He's far from well and he does expect to see me.'
That was true, although her uncle would have under-
stood if her job had taken her away for a few days.

But she wanted to spend this break with Marc. They
had not been out together again but she had high
hopes for the days and nights they would be alone.

Elsie spent Sundays with her sister, and today Robin
had prepared a light lunch for Maybelle, Marc and
herself. Now Maybelle was resting, Marc was on the
phone in his study, and Robin was getting coffee for
him and herself when she heard a car draw up and
Dominic strolled into the kitchen.

He was in a pale blue tracksuit and trainers, and he
looked hot and flushed. Marc always seemed cool but
Dominic obviously felt the heat. 'Warm enough for
you?' he enquired.

'Just about,' said Robin. 'Coffee?'

'No, thanks.' He took a can of something from the
fridge, snapped it open and gulped a little, then sat
down and looked at Robin. 'So what's the latest?' he
asked. 'I hear you're not off to Bournemouth with
Maybelle. What are you going to do with yourself?'

'She's leaving me some work.'

'When you get bored give me a ring; we'll go out for
a drink.'

'You will bring Lucy?' Robin said sweetly, and
Dominic grinned.

'Spoilsport. And you,' he said to Marc, who had just
walked in.

'I thought I heard you,' said Marc. 'Is this a social
call or what?'

'It's always a bonus getting an eyeful of this gorgeous

girl,' said Dominic, 'but I came to ask if you're coming Wednesday night; do we get another ticket?'

'You do if we're coming,' said Marc. He looked at Robin. 'What do you feel about culture with cucumber sandwiches?'

'What with what?' said Robin.

'Give her a break,' said Dominic. 'It's *A Midsummer Night's Dream*—Shakespeare, you know—in the gardens of Hedway Manor. Then a champagne supper, dancing and cavorting. It's always a good do.'

It was an annual county charity affair, in an Elizabethan manor-house where the gardens were said to be fabulous. And the actors were all top names.

'It sounds very educational,' Robin joked.

'Another ticket, then,' said Dominic.

After Dominic had gone Marc said, 'You're driving to Bournemouth that day, settling them in, then driving back. I hope you won't be too tired for a party that could go on till dawn.'

She had always had loads of energy but he might be regretting having no choice about inviting her, and she asked, 'Did you want me to go with you?'

'If I go,' he said emphatically, 'I most certainly want you with me, but I had hoped for a less public place for our first night without Maybelle.'

After that she regretted not having pretended that she hated Shakespeare and had an allergy to champagne, but a fairy tale being played out in a magical garden would surely make it an enchanted evening.

On Wednesday morning, with her luggage in the boot, Maybelle was settled in the back seat of the car where her friend would be joining her. As Robin slipped in behind the wheel Marc said, 'Drive carefully, and get yourself back here safely. And to Maybelle he added, 'Have a good holiday; don't take up any more good causes and don't worry.'

'It's not you I worry about,' said Maybelle.

Nobody need worry about Marc, thought Robin; he could take care of himself. But she would worry about Dominic, maybe. Maybe about Robin a little. Maybelle had played the chaperon these last few days, being around most of the time when Robin and Marc might have been alone together. She didn't seem too happy about Robin going back to the house alone and, at the last minute, when Maybelle and her friend had had their luggage taken up to the comfortable room they always had in the hotel and Robin was turning to leave, Maybelle said, 'I'm going to miss you. Won't you stay? I'm sure they could find you a room, and sea air—'

'No, thank you,' Robin said quickly, and she had to check herself from rushing off and go on walking out of the room at a normal rate.

'Robin,' Maybelle called as she reached the doorway.

'Yes?'

'Nothing.' Maybelle gave one of her little smiles and her little shrugs. 'Just take care.'

'Of course,' said Robin. 'And you.'

She got out of the hotel fast, into Maybelle's car and away, with a marvellous sense of freedom and escape. It was a warm day and she wound the sun-roof right back, the windows right down. And the wind streamed through her long hair as she sang in her off-key voice the steamiest love songs she could remember.

More than anything she would have liked to spend the evening and the night all alone with Marc, but the evening could still be entertaining. It was a society affair, always covered in the pages of glossy magazines, with men in evening dress, women in high fashion, and at the very least she would have something to tell her friends.

She had spoken on the phone to some of them, and they knew about her job but nothing about the way she felt about Marc. That was Robin's own lovely secret, and if she had had money to spare she might have bought a madly expensive outfit to compete with the haute-couture set. But she was fond of the dress she had decided on, and she would be beautiful because she would be with Marc.

She had nothing to do but get ready when she got back. Marc was not home yet. Elsie was watching television in the little sitting room that led off the larger drawing room. 'You left them, then?' said Elsie as Robin reached the open door.

'They'll be all right, won't they?'

'Oh, they'll be all right,' said Elsie. 'You off to this do tonight, then?'

'Yes.'

'Some of them won't be too pleased to see you—that Leila, for one.'

Robin had not seen Leila again. That didn't mean that Marc hadn't seen her, or that they hadn't spoken on the phone, but so far as Robin knew she had not come to the house again. So Leila would be with the party and she wouldn't want Robin joining them, but Robin was too happy to let it spoil her anticipation.

Her dress had been a bargain find in a nearly new shop a few months ago. It was simple, straight and short, in heavy silver lace, and her smooth arms and long, bare legs looked pale gold against it, like the few freckles on her nose.

She was sitting at the dressing table fiddling with her hair when Marc called, 'Robin?'

'Here,' she hollered back.

'Half an hour to go.'

She had combs and slides and she went on experimenting until she'd made a centre parting, clipping back one side of her hair with a silvery slide and letting the other side fall in loose waves. Then she looked at her shoes, hovering between her new patent leather pumps and a pair of silver strappy sandals that had seen better days. She should have resprayed the sandals but it was too late for that now, and she went downstairs, carrying both pairs, towards the full-length mirror in the downstairs cloakroom.

Before she reached the hall she knew that Marc was down here. She couldn't hear him or see him but she went to the drawing room and there he was, uncoiling from one of the armchairs, very distinguished in the classic black and white of evening dress.

'You look stunning, as always,' he said. She had been told that often but now it seemed like the first time, almost making her blush, and she held out two pairs of shoes.

'Which do I wear? The silver are scuffed.'

'A pity you have to wear shoes,' he said, and she pulled a laughing face.

'I'll need them if there's dancing.' The last time she had had her toes trodden on, and she wondered if he remembered that.

He was smiling when he said, 'A pity you have to—' and left the sentence unfinished.

Wear anything? Later, she thought, and smiled at the shared intimacy, safe and happy.

She decided for herself on the sandals. 'Maybe the scuffs won't show.'

She slipped them on and fastened the straps and Marc said, 'Have a drink before we pick up Dominic and Lucy.'

'Are you having one?'

'I'm driving, but there's no reason why you shouldn't.'

He was pouring her something, and although she felt fine she would be meeting strangers who were not her friends. She sipped the vodka and tonic, and wondered if Marc thought she might need a small confidence-booster.

When she asked, 'Do I need this? Are there going to be any of them whose feathers I can ruffle by saying hardly anything?' he smiled again.

'With your flair for stirring it I'm promising nothing.'

But she was causing no trouble tonight. She was going to be so well behaved, and if Leila was bitchy again Robin would understand why this time. She was sorry for Leila because Marc was with Robin and Robin was so happy that nothing could hurt her.

Dominic and Lucy's apartment was in a block of luxury flats with lawns running down to the river. As Marc drew up near the entrance someone waved from a first-floor window, and in a few minutes they both came out.

Lucy's hair was shining like spun silk and her white dress was frilled and flounced. Marc was out of the car, taking Lucy's hand, and when she dimpled up at him he must have been telling her how enchanting she looked. Because she did, like a fairy-tale princess.

She got into the seat behind Robin with a rustle of skirts and with Dominic beside her. 'You haven't met Robin,' said Dominic. Robin turned and Lucy's smile was wistful.

She said, 'I've seen you before, around town. I always thought you had to be a model.'

'Gosh, no,' said Robin. She had had modelling offers, but all with strings attached that had made them less than tempting. She said, 'That's a lovely dress.' It must have cost a fortune, and it made Robin wonder if her second-hand bargain was suitable after all. Especially when Dominic leaned over and leered.

'I must say, my darling, your little number is a winner, what there is of it.'

Marc raised an eyebrow. After that Robin tried to pull her skirt down another couple of inches over her bare knees.

When they arrived cars were already filling the courtyard of the manor-house, where people were rushing around, greeting friends, and a quick survey told Robin that her dress was fine. Although there was a sprinkling of ballgowns there were silk suits, trouser suits, dresses, some outfits outlandish enough for the catwalk, all looking very pricey. But Robin's silver sheath was elegant enough when she stood tall and straight.

Leila was there. She must have been waiting for their car because she was almost beside it when it stopped, and as Marc and Dominic got out she made straight for Marc. She could have kissed him for all Robin knew because Robin didn't stop to see. She opened her own door, slipped out of her seat and looked away from Marc and Leila. If they kissed she didn't want to see.

As Dominic helped Lucy out and she started fluffing her frills into place, Leila and Marc came round the car and Leila gave Robin a long, slow glare. Then she hooted with laughter. 'You've got to be understudying Cobweb.'

She meant one of the fairy queen's attendants. The lace *was* cobwebby, but Leila was out for a quick laugh at Robin's expense.

'Robin's too tall for a fairy,' said Dominic. 'How about Puck?'

'I can't see Robin saying, "Fear not, my lord, your servant shall do so,"' said Marc.

'It wouldn't come easily,' said Robin, and now although they were smiling nobody was laughing at her.

'Where *did* you get it?' Leila asked.

'I spun it myself,' Robin said cheerfully. 'They don't call me Spiderwoman for nothing.'

No one else was unfriendly. Everyone who knew the Hammonds—and almost everybody seemed to—accepted Robin being in their group, although there was probably talk about her having arrived with Marc Hammond.

From the courtyard they passed through the great hall into the gardens, to tiered seats and a wide stage of lawns and trees. They were transported to a forest where fairies lived and humans were bewitched, and Robin sat with Marc. Every seat was taken, but for her there was only Marc, beside her, and the play was magical. No man-built theatre could have given this illusion. She was enchanted with it all. She sat, leaning forward, chin in her hand, drinking in the words and the music. Night had fallen in the wood but the arc-lights made moonlight as Puck and Oberon touched the sleepers' eyes with the little purple flower that was a love spell.

When they woke they were deep in love, and Robin looked up at Marc's profile and thought, It can happen that fast. As she raised her face he turned his head and tilted her chin and kissed her gently, and she was bewitched, besotted, caught in the spell.

She was sorry when the play ended, the actors took their bows and the forest became a garden again. Marc said, 'Penny for your thoughts?' because Robin was still gazing towards the trees.

'I thought that was magic,' she said.

'Let's get some champagne,' said Dominic. 'These seats get harder every year.' And Robin snapped out of her dreamy mood. The fantasy was over. Marc had brought her to a party as well as a play, and soon she was enjoying herself because this was a very good party.

With Marc beside her, her striking looks got her noticed, and her zip and zest made most of the folk she was meeting like her. As always she was attracting attention and adding to the gaiety of the gathering.

In a vast dining room, where champagne was flowing and tables were covered with exotic edibles, some of the women had begun eyeing her, wondering how things were between Marc Hammond and that girl. So had some of the men, wondering what their own chances were because she looked like a natural party-goer. Robin could have told them not to bother, that they would be wasting their time.

'Watch that one,' Lucy warned her as a man with a pointed nose and gingery whiskers came towards them, his eyes on Robin. 'He's one of the huntin', shootin' set and he thinks he's God's gift.'

'From the look of him I'd expect him to be running with the fox,' Robin hissed back, and when he reached them both girls were giggling.

With Marc, Lucy and Dominic, Robin stayed in a spot by a high, many-paned window in the dining room, while the company eddied around them. Leila was almost as close to Marc as Robin was, and while strangers were speaking to Robin Marc and Leila were talking to each other. Robin could only half hear. It didn't seem to be anything much that they were talking about, but she did catch a wry look that Leila gave him, as if something was going on, and Robin gulped her champagne and took another glass from a passing tray.

She was not jealous. Of course she wasn't. Although she wished that Leila would stop smiling at Marc as if they were sharing a joke, or a secret.

Someone was asking, 'How long have you known the Hammonds?'

'I know Maybelle Myson best,' Robin answered, and wondered if that could be true. She knew that she was crazy about Marc but there had to be so much she didn't know about him.

But it was a very good party. Dancing was in the great hall, with its stone fireplace big enough to drive a bus in, and the carved coat of arms above. And a group was playing in the minstrels' gallery. This had been used as a ballroom for generations and there was a ball being held here tonight.

Robin danced. There were a dozen or so round the Hammonds' table and she danced with all the men but Marc. Marc was not dancing. When she asked him he said, 'After the last time I wouldn't inflict that on you again.'

She had thought that last time was fantastic and knew he was joking, but Dominic jumped up. 'If you're asking I'm dancing.'

'All right?' she asked Lucy.

'Don't ask me,' said Lucy.

Dominic was not bad at all. He stepped out nimbly and Robin whirled around with the best of them. She had always found dancing a release and she went with the music, letting it take her into the rhythm, sometimes with Dominic, sometimes with whoever she found herself facing.

Then back to the table, to ices and cold drinks—and Marc, who smiled when she came back and looked handsome as the devil, but would not dance with her.

'Do you mind?' she asked him when Foxy-face came up and asked her to dance.

'Of course not,' Marc said. 'Enjoy yourself.'

She was, in a way. But she had stopped drinking champagne a while ago, and she didn't want to leave Marc sitting by Leila—who didn't seem to want to dance either.

Foxy-face was an awful bore, and he was one of those clutch-them-tight dancers. He held Robin in a sweaty grasp, breathing boozy fumes on her face while he was asking why the most sensational girl here tonight wasn't in show business.

'Nobody's asked me,' said Robin, and that was a mistake because he had a producer friend who might just have the right part for her. If she'd like to meet Foxy for dinner one night they could discuss it.

'I'll bet,' she muttered. 'I'd have to ask my lawyer,' she said.

'Marc Hammond? You came with the Hammonds?'

'I came with Marc. I am with Marc.'

'My mistake,' said Foxy. 'We wouldn't want to upset Marc Hammond, would we? Tell you what. You square it with him and give me a bell.'

After that dance, and receiving a whiskery kiss which she managed to dodge getting full on the lips, she went up onto the gallery, along to a palatial retiring room, to wash hands and splash the kiss from her cheek.

No more dancing for her tonight. If she was tired, perhaps Marc would take her home—if she could get Leila's clutching fingers off his arm.

Earlier she had been so sure that nothing could go wrong, and nothing had. Except that Marc seemed to be distancing himself while Robin was being whirled around on a carousel. That was her own fault. She should have stayed put. And she might have done if she hadn't had the champagne.

The silvery hair-slide was slipping. She unclipped it and ran her fingers through her hair. She might look wilder now but she felt better. She held her wrists under the cold tap again and ran the water until the coolness spread up her arms.

A couple of women in here were watching her, and as she walked out of the room another came in. Just outside the door Leila was leaning against a pillar, waiting for Robin.

'Congratulations,' said Leila.

'What?'

'Hugo says he's getting you a film test.'

With anyone else Robin would have laughed and said, Want to bet it would mean stripping off? But with Leila she could only shake her head.

'How does it feel to have all the men making fools of themselves over you?' Leila asked, and before

Robin could speak, Leila answered herself, 'Well, not all of them, I suppose. Dominic, of course—he never stops raving about you. You've got poor little Lucy worried sick and so, as usual, she runs to Marc with her troubles.' Robin's throat was suddenly dry as dust.

'Well, Marc can stop worrying now,' said Leila. 'You've done it for him—shown Dominic that you're anybody's, that is.'

Without warning the group started up again, with a crash like thunder, hurting Robin's head. The coolness of the water on her wrists seemed to have seeped into her veins, turning her blood to ice.

Leila was as vicious as Aunt Helen, but what Leila was saying could make sense. Marc might be stringing Robin along to stop her getting her claws into Dominic. She didn't want to believe that but it could be happening. She couldn't think clearly. There was too much noise, too many people.

What had she done tonight? Nothing very awful, surely? She'd danced, while Marc had sat back watching her, as Aunt Helen would have said, 'making a spectacle' of herself. She shoved her hair away from her face with both hands, and looked at Leila, clearing the blur from her vision. Leila's smirk might represent how most of them tonight were seeing her. How Marc was seeing her.

She came down the great staircase, head high, walking with a dancer's grace between the dancers, towards the table where Marc was sitting with others.

If he had watched them on the gallery he might have guessed what Leila had been saying. His face was unreadable, telling her nothing.

Heaven help me, she thought, sick at heart; whose tune have I been dancing to?

CHAPTER SEVEN

THERE was one way of finding out what was going on. Marc might be impossible to read but Dominic was an open book, and Robin looked at Dominic now, giving him the full battery of a radiant smile and fluttering her long dark lashes. 'Would you risk dancing with me again?' she invited, and Dominic leapt out of his seat.

He was a born flirt and he probably did have a crush on her. She knew that over-eagerness. When Dominic reached for her she saw the pleading look Lucy gave Marc, as if she was begging him, Please stop them. Leila had said that Lucy ran to Marc with her problems and that made sense. It was what Robin herself had done.

She would always be grateful that he had helped to save Uncle Edward's life and got her through that terrible night. To Robin it had all seemed intimate and personal, but she couldn't know if that was how Marc had seen it.

The next morning Maybelle had said, 'There's nobody like Marc in an emergency,' and when Robin had gushed, 'He was wonderful,' Maybelle had said wryly, 'He often is. That could be why women make fools of themselves over him.'

Maybelle had warned her. Maybelle had been worried about going away and leaving Robin behind, because she had guessed that Robin was falling for a man who would hurt her. Maybelle knew Marc, and she could have suspected he was flattering Robin to stop her responding to Dominic's flattery.

He *could* have been. He hadn't looked lover-like just now. He'd looked more as he had that first evening when he'd told her, 'Watch it. . .because I shall be watching you and I rarely miss a trick.'

Even in the crush of the dancers she was sure Marc's eyes were on them as she smiled across at Dominic, asking him, 'Do you get this feeling we're being watched?'

'You always are,' he said.

'Not always by your brother and your girlfriend.'

Dominic grinned sheepishly.

Robin was weary of bright lights, tired of pretending a gaiety she was no longer feeling. As they came to an open door, through which guests were strolling and dancing onto lawns, she said, 'I need air,' and danced herself and her partner outside.

It was less crowded out here and the lights were gentler. They danced in silence and Dominic's touch did nothing to her. Marc's touch had been electric, but Marc had never looked at her with anything like Dominic's expression of dog-like devotion.

Through an archway in a hedge they reached a much smaller lawn, where only one couple wandered, hand in hand, and Dominic stopped dancing to say, 'You know I'm mad for you, don't you?'

'It's the champagne.'

'No, it i-isn't. You're sensational, Robin, you know that.'

So Foxy had just told her, but he had simply been a conceited man on the make, while Dominic was stumbling over his words as if he believed what he was saying—and Lucy might well be worried, although she had nothing in the world to fear from Robin.

Robin said, 'Lucy's very pretty.'

'What?' It was as though he had forgotten Lucy's name.

'And you're getting married in October.'

'We're supposed to be.'

Robin's hair was falling in a dark cloud around the pale cameo of her face and Dominic said huskily, 'I could go for you in a big way, Robin; I could go all the way for you.' His hands were shaking on her shoulders, and they were nothing like Marc's hands. And if he kissed her it would be nothing, and she was sorry for Dominic and sorry for herself.

She said, 'You're not being fair to Lucy,' and he shrugged Lucy away. 'And what would Marc have to say?'

'I don't know,' said Dominic. 'I don't care.'

'I'm here with Marc.'

He gave a jeering yelp. 'Don't kid yourself, darling; you're not here with Marc. Leila is with Marc, and the reason he's keeping a tight rein on you is because I might ask you to run away with me.'

So their stories tallied, Leila's and Dominic's. Both were telling her she was being manipulated like a puppet on a string—and she could have run amok through this gentrified county set, screaming her head off until she reached Marc Hammond. And then, Lord knows what she would have done, except go on screaming and hit him with the nearest blunt instrument.

Instead she laughed, quite musically, and said, 'Do you want to run away with me?' and thought, That would show Marc. But that would hurt Maybelle and Lucy and I wouldn't want that. 'Joke,' she said.

'Is it?' said Dominic, and Robin's laughter was holding back tears. The only time she had really wept Marc had taken her in his arms, and she had looked at him and thought she was in love. Like the humans when the fairies crept near them with the purple flower.

There were flowers here, in antique grey stone urns, their colours drained by the moonlight, but some could have been dark red or purple, and Robin said, 'I loved the play; didn't you love the play? What was that flower—love-in-idleness?'

'I don't know,' said Dominic. He watched her in her gleaming silver dress as she plucked a flower. She didn't want him to touch her or tell her how much he wanted her, or she might start screaming. At Dominic. At Marc. At the crazy torment her life was turning into.

The music still reached them and she began to sway to its rhythm. Dancing fast was the next best thing to screaming for unravelling the knot of misery in her stomach. She danced to the fiercer beat in her brain, arms flung wide, hair swirling, twirling around like a dervish on the little lawn, until the stars whirled overhead and she was so dizzy that she staggered when Dominic gripped her arm.

Only it wasn't Dominic, it was Marc, and she tried to jerk back and keep upright until the world stopped spinning.

'Time to go home,' said Marc. 'High time, by the looks of you.'

He thought she was high on champagne. The wild child, born to cause trouble. And maybe from that

very first drink, before they'd even met up with Lucy
and Dominic, Marc had wanted Dominic to see her
making such a spectacle of herself.

But she was not high. She was dizzy from dancing
but she was cold sober and seeing everything clearly
for the first time in days. Marc Hammond most of all,
with his hooded eyes and the curve to his mouth that
was no smile. How could she have trusted him so
blindly when he was such a deep and secret man?

It had been like a spell. She opened her clenched fist
where the flower lay on her palm, and quoted brightly,
'"The juice of it on sleeping eyelids laid Will make or
man or woman madly dote Upon the next live creature
that it sees. Maidens call it love-in-idleness."'

'No, they don't,' said Marc. 'They call it petunia and
I don't advise rubbing it into anyone's eyes. We're
leaving. Lucy has a headache, and if you don't have
one yet you'll probably have a hangover in the
morning.'

'Aren't you the considerate one?' mocked Robin. 'I
suppose you wouldn't consider taking Lucy home and
leaving us here?'

'You suppose right,' Marc said curtly. 'Come on.'
He turned away and Robin pressed her fingertips to
her lips to stop them trembling. It was like that time
with Tony. 'Right, you two—in my office,' Marc
Hammond had commanded, and meekly they had
followed, just as Robin and Dominic were following
him now.

Marc Hammond was still in command—or thought
he was, because Dominic was saying softly, 'Will you
meet me tomorrow night?'

'What?' Robin couldn't take her eyes off Marc, who

was not even turning back to check that they were following. He was that sure they were.

'Seven o'clock. The Fishermen's Field. Will you come?' Dominic whispered.

She wondered how Marc would have reacted if she hadn't gone into her whirl-around and had let Dominic kiss her, and Marc had come upon them seriously necking. He would have been even more caustic. Break it up, he would have said. But then it would still have been, We're going home. There would have been no fuss because deep down he was always the iceman. Nothing stirred him too deeply. And not for the first time she thought that before she got out of his life she would like to give ten years of her own life to get him ranting and raving.

'Will you come?' Dominic asked again, and now they were nearing the doorway that led out of the gardens into the great hall.

'Don't hold your breath,' said Robin.

Lucy could have had a headache. She was pale, but she smiled when they reached the table and said, 'I'm being a bore, aren't I?'

'Of course you're not,' Marc said. 'We've all had our money's worth for tonight.'

'Some of us certainly have,' Leila trilled, looking at Robin. 'I liked your hair better with the hair-clip in. Didn't you notice you'd lost it?'

Robin must have left the hair-slide in the retiring room. It had been cheap and cheerful, not worth going back for, and anyway Lucy was on her feet and they were saying goodnights.

Leila went out with them to where their cars were parked and her arm was through Marc's every step of the way. Leila was with Marc. Robin wasn't. Marc had

had Robin on a tight rein but there was no real bond between them, and, walking beside him now, Robin could have been miles away.

She would rather have sat on the back seat with Lucy. She would rather not have got into the car at all. But Marc had the passenger door open and a hand under Robin's elbow, and she had to slip in as he guided her unless she wanted to create a scene here and now. The scene would probably come. Because her eyes had been opened, and she was no longer under a spell. But she couldn't make one now, not with an audience like this around.

Some other cars were pulling away. Not many. The Hammonds were leaving early from an all-night party and Lucy waved to friends while Robin sat with her fingers gripped tightly together. As they came out of the courtyard into the tree-lined drive Lucy said in a bright little voice, 'Hugo Jarvis says he's introducing you to a film producer, Robin; have you done any acting?'

'No,' said Robin, although she was putting on a good act now, sitting sedately when she could have spat at Marc Hammond like an angry cat.

'Don't take everything Jarvis offers at face value,' said Marc. 'He's not always reliable.'

Robin gave a hoot of strangled laughter. 'I can't trust him, you mean? Well, I am very glad you warned me, because I'm such an idiot I'm always trusting two-timing rats.'

'That,' drawled Marc, 'could account for your colourful reputation.'

'Robin's a star,' Dominic said hastily. 'She was born for the spotlight.'

Marc laughed at him. 'When she needs a fan club

we'll let you know. And when you get home get some black coffee down you because you're in the office at nine in the morning.' He sounded amused, as if Dominic had had enough champagne to make anything he was saying ridiculous.

Perhaps he had, but he would probably be waiting by the river tomorrow night for Robin. He would be sober then, and if she didn't have such scruples she could take him away from Lucy, at least for a while— because Dominic was hooked on the way she looked, as others had been, and much good it had done her.

It was only a few miles to Marc Hammond's house after they put down Lucy and Dominic, but as soon as they drove away together alone in the car the strain of silence became too much for Robin and she heard herself say, 'That was quite an evening.'

'Yes, indeed,' Marc said drily, and she chattered on.

'One thing I've always wondered about in *A Midsummer Night's Dream*... . The spell was taken off one pair of lovers and they were back to normal, still in love like they'd always been. But the others—he'd hated the girl before, badly enough to want to kill her, and he was left under the spell. Suppose Puck, who had a weird sense of humour, had nipped back years later with the antidote? What would have happened then, when Demetrius stopped being bewitched?'

'It's a little late to ask Shakespeare.' Marc was still playing her along, laughing at her because he thought she was an airhead. Maybe she had been stupid where he was concerned, imagining she was special to him when, apart from putting on the charm, he had never committed himself in any way.

It had been easy for him. The first time Robin Johnson had been no trouble at all. Marc had only had to wine and dine her a little, talk, smile at her, sympathise with her for Robin, who had always been her own woman, to turn into putty in his hands.

Although she hadn't been in his hands that much. He hadn't made love to her; a brush of a kiss while they were watching the play didn't count. Dominic was mad for her. He would have risked making love in the gardens just now, where anyone could have walked by. But she had practically propositioned Marc—something she had never done to any man before. And he had turned her down so smoothly that she had believed him when he had said, Some other time.

What other time? How far would Marc go to keep her believing he cared about her, the outsider who could be a troublemaker? If she led him on, just to see how far he would go and then said, Sorry, but I think I'd prefer Dominic, anything that happened would be worth that triumph when the tables were turned and he was the one getting dumped.

Recklessness swept over her in the darkness of the car. Caution had never been her strong point and she wasn't showing much sense rushing into a headlong collision with Marc Hammond. But she was so sick with herself for being so easily fooled that she hardly cared what happened if only she could cut him down.

Elsie was in bed. A few lights burned and as they came into the kitchen Robin said, 'I'd love a coffee.'

'That might not be a bad idea.'

She didn't need sobering but she said, 'I'll be in the drawing room. Instant would be fine, just black and strong.'

'Right away.' He still sounded amused but he wouldn't be for long.

In the drawing room she kicked off her silver

sandals. There were green grass stains on them now and she remembered asking him which shoes she should wear. 'A pity you have to wear shoes,' he had said. A pity she had to wear anything. The dress was skimpy; she could slip out of it easily and then see how he would react.

Maybe he had intended to take things further tonight but it would not have been love he was offering. Just sensual and highly charged sex—another skill he'd be expert in. Men had pestered her for sex for years and she had wondered sometimes if she was frigid, because she had never lost her head and certainly not her heart. Tonight there was no danger of either, with a man who had betrayed her so brutally.

Marc brought two cups of coffee and she said, 'I wouldn't have thought you needed one; I didn't think you were drinking much.' How did she know that, unless she had watched him as much as he had watched her? And she couldn't have done because she was dancing.

He said, 'I'm a black-coffee addict.'

'Of course.' She sat down, her bare legs crossed, the silver dress slipping slightly from one shoulder. 'Dominic,' she said, 'doesn't seem to be keen on getting married.'

'Did he tell you that?' He was sitting opposite, the lawyer with a witness who might have something useful to tell, but she answered his question with another.

'Why should Lucy want to marry him if he doesn't want her?'

'I suppose because when he's not making a bloody fool of himself she finds him lovable.'

'And he's making a bloody fool of himself now?'

'He is if he doesn't realise you'd give him more trouble than he could handle.'

She was suddenly on her feet, and he was getting up and moving towards her. She said, 'Dominic wants me. If I decided I wanted him you'd stop that, would you?'

'Yes.'

'How?'

He started to say something, she thought. His head was bowed just above her upturned face, and then all sound ceased except for the roaring in her ears, because somehow his mouth was on her mouth. His hands were behind her head and for a split second there was stillness.

Then he kissed her deeper, and everything in her responded as if a powder trail had reached flashpoint. As his lips traced a line along her collar-bone a fevered pulse leapt everywhere—in her throat, racing through the arteries of her blood, quickening her womb—and she knew so well what he was doing, making her moan and writhe, turning her body into a sensual eruption over which she had no control.

Or hardly any. Just enough to shake her head, with her hair weighing so heavily that it dragged her head back, and sob, 'No. . .' And incredibly he stopped, his lips on her breast, a hand low on her spine, holding her hard against him. He held her like that for a moment, then he moved away the half-step that could have set her free.

She knew there was something she had planned to say now, and she knew—she did know—why this had happened, and that for him it had been only a tightening of the rein. He would be a better lover than Dominic, better at everything than Dominic, and he would risk her falling in love with him because he could deal with that. It must have happened a few times before. Maybelle had known there would be pain for Robin if she let herself care too much for Marc.

Her dress had slipped down to her waist and so had her bra. She hitched them both up and gasped, 'Quite an evening.'

'Leave him alone,' Marc said, and she managed to cackle with laughter.

'Back to what it's all about? Do you expect me to say, Who? Am I supposed to have forgotten about Dominic after that little set-to?' She had to get out of the room and pull herself together behind a locked door.

'We'll talk in the morning,' Marc said.

A minute earlier he had been well on the way to seducing her on the floor in an orgy of unbridled passion. Now he was talking of talking, and it was too late to make a crack about turning him down because she fancied Dominic. He was still in control and she could only say, as coolly as she could manage, 'I'll really look forward to that.'

She was not looking forward to it. She was not looking forward to anything that would be happening to her tomorrow, and when she reached her darkened room she dropped full-length on the bed and waited for whatever rush of emotion was going to hit her next.

Mostly it was anger. She was enraged at the way she had been treated, at how he was still trying to treat her. And she was madder than ever at herself, because if he had gone on when she'd moaned no she would have been beyond resistance. Tomorrow they might talk about Dominic, but tonight she would have let Marc make love to her—only, it wouldn't have been love—because while her mind was warning her not to be a fool every other inch of her just wanted him terribly.

In the morning she would have a hangover. Not from the champagne, but it would be a black depression and it would hurt like death...

In the morning she talked to herself as she showered and dressed, telling herself that she shouldn't be surprised at what was happening. Marc Hammond was nowhere near the first man who had tried to take advantage of her, but he was the first she had fallen for. She couldn't laugh and shrug this off as she had done with others. For the first time she needed revenge, to wipe the slate clean, or she was going to be obsessed with him for ever.

When she went into the kitchen Morag had just arrived and was taking off her coat, and she and Elsie both wanted to hear about last night. 'Was it worth the money?' asked Morag.

Robin hadn't paid for her ticket, they'd know that, but she said, 'Worth it for the champagne alone.'

'Marc's in the study,' said Elsie. 'He said you were to go in as soon as you came down.'

It was later than Marc usually left for work, so he meant to see Robin before the day got under way. She tapped on the door and he called, 'Come in.'

He was working—he had papers and a pen so he wasn't wasting time—and he gave her a pleasant enough smile.

'Come and sit down,' he said. 'After last night perhaps we should discuss Dominic.'

She sat and waited, acutely conscious of his movements, or rather his stillness—his hand on the typewritten page, the line of a white shirt-cuff edging a

darker jacket sleeve. He had to be breathing but his
shoulders were still and his face showed no flicker of
emotion. Then he asked her, 'What do you want from
life, Robin?'

That was a heck of a question. Yesterday he would
have been top of her list. Now she shrugged. 'The
usual things. Why?'

'Do you want to get into entertainment? If you do I
could introduce you to contacts who might be of help.'

'Not like Foxy—Hugo?'

'Not like Hugo.'

No strings, he meant, and that would be a change.
Modelling offers could get her away from here, and
out of sight would probably mean out of mind for
Dominic. She recrossed her legs, stretching slim ankles,
smiling. 'That's very tempting but I never wanted to
be a model, and I don't have the training to be an
actress.'

'Then, how much?'

That was no bigger insult than what had gone before.
All along he had been confident he could buy her off,
with charm or cash, and she said brightly, 'Do you
have to do much paying out to stop Dominic making,
as you put it, a bloody fool of himself?'

His smile was entirely cynical. 'He's always been a
pushover for a pretty face, but this is the first time
he's—'

'Made a spectacle of himself?' she suggested, and
got the inevitable eyebrow quirk. 'Just a phrase that
came into my mind,' she said airily. 'By the way, whose
money are we dealing with here? Who's paying? You
or Lucy?'

'Does it matter?'

No, it didn't; she was just saying anything. All she

wanted to do was make him sweat, and she put on a thoughtful expression. 'I'll have to consider this,' she said.

'You do that. In the meantime keep away from him.' He stood up as she got up to leave the room and she thought wildly, No one could fault him on common courtesy. And she wondered what would happen if she said, You name your figure; I'd like to know my nuisance value.

She could do no hanging around here today. After she heard his car leave she came down from her room and went out of the house through the front door. In the drive she passed the gardener. 'Mornin',' he said. 'Off for a walk?'

'A good long walk,' she said, and left him staring as she strode past him, because he had just seen Mr Hammond drive away and he hadn't looked too pleased with life either.

Robin walked the six miles to her friend's home along roads and lanes, getting a couple of offers of lifts—one from a stranger—but turning both down because she needed to kill time so that she arrived at Amy's mid-morning, a reasonable hour for visiting.

Amy—Robin's friend whom she helped at the Sunday market—and her two-year-old son lived with Amy's parents in a terraced cottage. Her mother opened the door, smiling when she saw Robin, because she liked the girl who had always been a good friend to Amy. 'Amy,' she called up the stairs, 'Robin's here.' And Amy came running down, all smiles too.

'Oh, smashing,' she said. She had had a dullish day ahead of her but Robin always put some zip into things. 'How long can you stay?'

'I've got the day off,' said Robin, giving up any idea

of unloading her troubles on Amy, because Amy was chattering happily.

'Come up and tell me about everything. Something exciting has got to have been happening to you.'

If Robin had said, I think my heart's broken because I feel quite dead inside, Amy wouldn't have wanted to believe her. Nothing got Robin down. Robin could always be relied on to cheer you up, and Amy almost danced back into her little bedsit, where Tommy was sitting on a rug with a pile of building bricks and Amy had been at work with her sewing machine.

'So, how's the job going?' she asked.

'All but gone,' said Robin, and laughed.

Most of her friends had heard by now that Robin was driving for Marc Hammond, and that was hardly likely to last, nor was being a companion to an elderly lady.

'What happened?' said Amy, and Robin shook her head.

'Clash of personalities. Remember the last time I worked at Hammond's?' Amy had been friends with Robin then, and knew how Robin had lost her first job, and that got her giggling and wondering, 'Whatever happened to Jack?'

'Haven't a clue,' Robin said cheerfully, 'but Marc Hammond hadn't forgotten either, and when his aunt wanted me as her live-in companion he was not a happy man.'

She *was* an actress or she couldn't have kept this up all day, being flip and funny as if she hadn't a care in the world. But it would have been worse being alone with her thoughts. Although Amy didn't know it, she was helping Robin hold back the time when she might well fall apart.

Uncle Edward didn't guess either, although he had to be the one who knew Robin best. He was improving visibly every day, and when she reached the hospital that evening his face looked fuller and firmer. 'How's my girl?' he asked her, and smiled as if there was a joke somewhere in that.

She told him, 'Not bad, but I'm leaving my job.'

'Can't say I'm sorry,' he said. 'I've every reason to thank Marc Hammond but—well, it's probably for the best.' He'd thought there was a chance Robin would be *too* grateful. No danger of that now, she thought, and tried to smile because he was chuckling.

'You're pleased with yourself,' she said. 'What a lot of cards you're getting.' She had brought in a bag of fruit but there was no need for it. He had a bowlful, several vases of flowers, and a stack of magazines.

'I can't get over how kind people are,' he said.

'They like you.' This had shown him how many folk did like him, and might have given him the self-esteem he lacked. So far, by luck, Robin had usually missed Aunt Helen, but Helen Hindley arrived daily, she knew. Now she asked, 'How's Aunt Helen taking it?' and Edward Hindley began to laugh.

'Come on,' she urged, 'tell me what she's been saying.'

'I don't know if I should.'

'We don't have secrets.'

She couldn't share her secret but it sounded right, and her uncle said, 'Well, your aunt came this afternoon, and when we were alone I told her, If Robin comes back, I said, you'll treat her right, because I won't have her hounded out of her home again.'

Robin hugged him. 'That was so brave of you. What did she say?'

'Well—' he was suddenly serious '—this was what I wasn't sure about telling you. She said she'd always known you were my daughter.' As Robin gasped he went on, 'No, my dear, no. I told Helen she was mistaken, but that that was the nicest thing she'd said to me in years.'

There was a lump in Robin's throat as she told him, 'You're the only father I've ever had and the only one I'll ever need.'

After that she had to talk about cheerful things, like his coming out of hospital, being sensible and staying well. She would watch out for him herself but she hoped he would not be needing much professional care, because Marc Hammond's financial help would not be forthcoming now—unless she took cash for laying off Dominic. She couldn't really do that, but she might take a cheque, just to make Marc sign it, and then tear it up in front of him and tell him that little brother had never been at risk from her, so big brother need not have bothered to keep them apart.

Dominic amused her. He was a nice guy who wasn't being too bright at the moment. She liked Dominic, but big brother was another matter—and 'nice' was not the word for him.

When she came out of the hospital she was still smouldering with resentment against Marc, who thought he was still telling her what to do. 'Keep away from him,' had been Marc's last words to her this morning, and she was in such a seething state of rebellion that she would have defied any order he gave.

Keep away from Dominic meant don't go to meet him, and she went from the hospital to the taxi rank and asked the driver to drop her just along the road from the Fishermen's Field.

It was not yet dark but most of the fishermen would have gone from this stretch of the tow-path. Lovers, dog-walkers and joggers sometimes parked in the meadow, but usually it emptied as it grew darker.

Dominic might not turn up. Robin had given the impression she wouldn't be coming herself, and it was entirely owing to Marc that she was trudging along until she turned off the road into the entrance to the Fishermen's Field.

There was only one car parked, a sports number that had to be Dominic's, and he got out of it as she came nearer. If he puts his hands on me, she thought, I shall shove him off his feet. But he didn't touch her. He reached out a hand then let it drop to his side and said, 'You came.'

'Looks like it,' she said.

She shouldn't have come. This was behaving stupidly. She had nothing to say to him and nothing he could say would interest her, and suddenly she was feeling so tired that the two-mile walk back into town seemed too far. Dominic would have to give her a lift back.

He opened the car door and she got in, and he sat beside her, looking at her. Then he said hoarsely, 'You are the most beautiful girl I've ever seen.'

She had heard it all before. So had most girls, she reckoned, when a man was trying to bed them.

Then Dominic asked, 'Would you go away with me? To Paris? A weekend in Paris?'

It sounded like the title of an old song, and she said wearily, 'I'm getting some smashing offers today. A weekend in Paris, and, from Marc, a blank cheque if I'll leave you alone.'

Dominic groaned, and it was so absurd that she couldn't resist a bad joke. 'I wonder if I could take them both—cash the cheque and then go to Paris? Only it couldn't be this weekend because a cheque takes how long to clear?'

Dominic shot up in his seat, as if someone had him by the throat. 'For God's sake, don't try cheating Marc.'

'I was joking.' Of course she was, although Marc would have cheated her—he *had* cheated her. But, reassured, Dominic smiled, and Robin said gently, 'You don't want to get involved with me.'

'Oh, but I *do*. Will you come? Do you have a passport?'

'Yes, I have a passport.'

'We could get a late flight tomorrow.'

'And be back before anyone misses us?'

'I wouldn't care if they did so long as nobody found out in time to stop us.'

This was getting crazier. She started to shake her head and he begged, 'Don't say no. Don't say anything. I'll get the tickets. Where will you be tomorrow?'

'At the house, I suppose.' She had work she should be doing—unfinished business for Maybelle.

'I'll come for you. Marc will be up north over the weekend.' So she wouldn't have to see Marc again and that was a relief, because she wasn't feeling just tired, she was bone-weary, as if the strain of last night and today had turned her into an old woman. Tomorrow she would say she was going nowhere with Dominic but she couldn't argue now—she could hardly find the energy to speak.

'Drive me back to the house, would you?' she said.
'And I'd be glad if you'd be quiet, because I have had
a very trying day and I need to get in touch with my
karma.'

Heaven knew what that was supposed to be, but it
kept Dominic quiet. She put her head back on the
headrest and closed her eyes and wished she could tap
into tranquillity. And if he looked at her he probably
thought she was spaced out, because when the car
stopped he said, 'Robin?' gently, as though he were
waking a sleepwalker. 'We're here, Robin.'

He had parked in the road where the car wouldn't
be seen from the house. She opened her door before
he could lean across her, and said, 'Thanks.'

'I'll come for you tomorrow. Say six o'clock.'

'You should be taking Lucy to Paris,' she said, and
walked away down the long, curved drive without
hearing what else he was trying to say.

The house didn't look welcoming tonight, but she
wanted to get into the little room that had been hers.
She could rest there and get back her strength because
she was really feeling rotten, almost ill. After always
taking health and vitality for granted it would be ironic
if she was sickening for something now.

She let herself in very quietly, with the front doorkey
that Maybelle had given her. Going through a side-
door, she would be more likely to meet somebody.
This way she might creep upstairs unseen.

But as she tiptoed towards the stairs Marc came into
the hall, and she knew before he said it that he was
going to demand, 'Where have you been?'

At the sight of him the blood went rushing to her
head and coursing through her veins. Dominic, who
was warm and human, left her cold and weary, while

this iceman brought her violently back to life, whooshing her right into fighting form.

'Give you three guesses,' she taunted. 'But, of course, you don't need three.' She kept on going towards the stairs with a smug little smile on her face. 'And I know you ordered me to keep away from him, but it may surprise you to hear that he doesn't seem able to keep away from me.'

He made no move at all to stop her. 'Why should it surprise me?' he drawled. 'Apart from Lucy, Dominic's taste in women has always been moronic. He's fascinated with you because you look like a tramp and you act like a tramp.'

The smile felt pinned to her lips, so that it hurt to hold it there, but through the pain she managed to say, 'Now, where have I heard that before?'

She got up the stairs, into her room and across to the dressing table and the mirror, with a red haze in front of her eyes as the hair fell over her face.

When she'd been thirteen, wearing her hair loose, Aunt Helen had shrieked, 'You're turning into a right little tramp.' She had called Robin a tramp many times since then and Robin had always got noticed; she was stared at, and Marc was not surprised that Dominic was hooked on her because she looked like a hooker.

She hated the way she looked. She hated the reflection that stared back at her, with the wild eyes and the flaming hair.

She jerked open a drawer, rooting among the contents, found scissors and began to lop off her hair. She hacked through the thickness until it was a jagged shoulder-length, then gathered up the long strands that had fallen around her and stumbled down the staircase, anger half blinding her.

The drawing-room door was open, and that was where Marc was, and when she stormed into the room the haze cleared because, for the first time, she was seeing Marc Hammond looking poleaxed. 'Bloody hell,' he gasped.

She had shaken him. She had cracked his control for a minute or two and staggered him. 'I don't believe it,' he said. 'Are you drunk?'

She must have had a slight brainstorm but that wasn't what he meant, and she said, 'No, and I wasn't last night either. I should have done this before, when I promised to cut my hair if Uncle Edward got better. You said it wouldn't make much difference but I think it does. Less hair should mean less of a tramp.'

There was such a lot of it as the silky skeins slid through her fingers onto the carpet. 'Good grief,' he said in a strangled voice, and she thought he was going to start laughing at her, and that if she didn't get out of the room before he did she might well stab him with the scissors.

CHAPTER EIGHT

BACK in her room, Robin's legs gave way. She collapsed on the stool in front of the dressing table and stared at her reflection. She looked terrible, wilder than ever, her hair like a burning bush.

Marc Hammond had made her do this. She was still dancing to his tune, without a mind of her own, and she had to get away from him. Far away would be safest, where she would no longer be looking for him the way she had for years. As soon as Uncle Edward was stronger she would leave this town and tomorrow she would go back to the house that used to be her home. Perhaps Aunt Helen would be less vindictive if her husband had convinced her that he had never been her sister's lover, and Aunt Helen at least should be pleased to see that the waist-length hair was now an unruly bob.

Elsie came into the room, stopped and pursed her lips. 'Whatever did you want to go and do this for?'

'I—got tired of it,' Robin said.

'Was it something Marc said?' Elsie asked

'No, goodness, *no*,' Robin said wildly. 'What could have given you that idea?'

'Mmm,' said Elsie, and after a moment added, 'You should have gone to a hairdresser.'

Robin agreed there. 'I've got a friend who might come in early in the morning and have a go at it if I ask her.'

'You phone her,' said Elsie, but before she went out

of the room she said, 'It's still very nice hair,' and Robin thought that was kind of her.

She rang on the telephone in Maybelle's room and wished that Maybelle were there. Not that Robin could have explained anything to her, but having Maybelle around would have steadied Robin and now she wouldn't even get the chance to say goodbye.

Sandy answered. She was another local girl who had known Robin most of her life, and when Robin asked, 'Would you do me a favour?' she said,

'You know I will if I can.'

'Would you come out here before you open the salon tomorrow and do my hair?' said Robin.

'Sure, but it'll take a time.' Sandy had trimmed ends and set Robin's hair for occasions.

'There's less of it now,' said Robin. 'I've just cut it.'

'You never have.' But Sandy was rarely surprised by what Robin got up to—Robin was full of surprises. She promised to be along in the morning, with her bag of equipment, and Robin thanked her and put down the phone.

Through the open door into the bedroom Maybelle Myson's bed was smooth under a cream silk counterpane. 'Goodnight,' Robin said softly. 'Sleep well.'

She could never come back to this house but she might see Maybelle again on her charity stall. She would have liked a photograph to take away, although she would never forget the woman she had pretended was her grandmother. She seemed to have known Maybelle a long time, but not as long as she had known Marc, although Robin would be doing her damnedest to forget him.

* * *

She slept badly and felt light-headed next morning with the weight of her hair gone. She was standing at a window in Maybelle's room that overlooked the front gardens when Sandy's old Morris Minor came down the drive, and Robin was downstairs opening the door as Sandy climbed out of the car.

Sandy was plump and pretty, with dark, bobbing curls and big brown eyes that went very wide when she saw Robin's hair.

'It was a snap decision,' said Robin, 'but I think it needs the professional touch.'

'You can say that again,' said Sandy. 'Lovely house,' she added as they went up the stairs, and when Robin opened the door of her room Sandy gave an appreciative, 'Ooh, I like this.'

'Me too,' said Robin, 'but I can't see myself staying.'

'What's happened?'

Robin told her what she had told Amy. 'I had a bust-up with Marc Hammond.'

Sandy laughed. Then she got down to the serious business of what to do with Robin's hair. She was good at her job, and although this presented a challenge it was still thick and silky and a fabulous colour. 'Any idea how you want it?' Sandy asked.

'Do what you can with it,' Robin said.

'Where's the hair you cut off?'

'Gone,' said Robin. Marc would have called Elsie in and told her to clear it away, and Elsie would have swept it into a newspaper and put it in the rubbish bin.

Robin felt that that was the place for it although Sandy wailed, 'You should have kept it; it would have made a fantastic hair-piece.'

Robin had already washed her hair and Sandy began shaping and layering, taking it back from Robin's face and telling her, 'You could wear any style with your cheekbones.'

During the blow-drying Sandy chattered happily, because she was creating something really super here. The shorter style, which would swing across Robin's cheek when she moved her head, showed the bone structure of her face, and that her eyes slanted slightly, fringed with long dark lashes, still with the green glint that Robin's eyes always had.

'How about that?' asked Sandy, stepping aside at last. She produced a hand-mirror from her bag to show Robin the back of her head and the skilful styling.

'You are clever,' Robin said admiringly, and Sandy began to pack up the tools of her trade.

'Oh, I'm clever,' she said, 'and you're a nut. Don't start cutting it yourself again.'

Robin promised. One brainstorm was enough. Marc Hammond would never make her act so crazily again. He was out of her life now, unless she could come up with some way of getting her own back that wouldn't be a two-edged sword. He had left early. Robin had heard his car go and sighed—with relief, of course, because if he was away for the weekend that meant she need never see him again.

After she'd waved goodbye to Sandy she went into the kitchen, where Elsie and Tom were having a morning cup of tea. 'Very nice,' Elsie said. 'Doesn't her hair look nice, Tom?'

'Aye,' said Tom.

'You are all right?' Elsie asked shrewdly. 'Your uncle's coming on all right?'

'I'm fine,' Robin lied, 'and he's doing very well, but this will be my last day here.'

'I thought you suited Maybelle,' said Elsie.

'But I didn't suit Marc.' She wondered if Elsie knew about Dominic, what had been going on, because Elsie nodded, as if there was nothing more to be said but also as if she was sorry.

At least Robin would leave things shipshape for Maybelle. She worked hard and fast on the typing she had been left. She made lists of appointments, mainly for charities, brought papers up from the bureau drawers and got notes that Maybelle had made into order.

The photograph of Marc Hammond on top of the bureau looked out at her and she asked it, 'Happy now?' She felt like dropping a heavy glass paperweight on top of it and leaving a note—Sorry about this. Do get the glass replaced and send me the bill. But he would know it was no accident.

Elsie brought her sandwiches at midday and Robin made herself eat although she was not hungry. In the early evening she packed her case and, all alone in the house, went into Maybelle's room for the last time to say a silent goodbye.

She had already said goodbye to Elsie, who was off to spend the evening with friends.

Then she carried her case downstairs, and before she rang for a taxi she went into the garden. It had begun to rain, not heavily but in a fine mist, although when she went into the little copse she was sheltered under the trees. There was a seat here under the horse-chestnut tree, and she sat there for a little while.

She had come out into the garden after the row when they'd got back late from the Nun's Well. She had been indignant, annoyed, and she had walked under the trees, muttering a few of the things she would have liked to say to Marc Hammond, ending with, I wouldn't fancy you if you were the last man on earth. And she'd smiled at herself because he'd made her mad but it hadn't mattered.

Now it was different. The anger was deeper, but it was the hurt that seemed like a mortal blow, so that when she got up and walked back towards the house her feet dragged. All she had to do now was phone for the taxi and see if Aunt Helen would let her in.

Back in the house she was at the phone in the hall, looking up the number of a taxi rank, when she heard a sound from the drawing room, and this time she was not prepared for Marc being there.

Even when she stood in the doorway, looking across to where he was standing, her face was stiff with surprise, and her, 'I wasn't expecting you back,' sounded squeaky.

'Not inconveniencing you, I hope,' he said, and that had to be sarcasm.

'Not really,' she said. 'Not particularly.'

She was hardly aware that she was moving into the room; it was as if she had stepped into a magnetic field with a pull she couldn't resist. But she had only taken a few steps before he said, 'The new hairstyle suits you.'

Then she stood still and said, 'Thank you.'

'Don't tell me you did this cut yourself.' He knew she hadn't.

'I rang a friend.'

'It's good to have friends.' Was he suggesting they could still be friends? Surely not after all that had been said? Although he would probably prefer a parting without fuss. Everything had gone his way; he could afford to be civilised.

She said, 'You won't forget Maybelle has to be collected early next week?'

'I'll see to it.'

And he could explain then why Robin had gone. If Maybelle phoned before, he could tell her. Robin hadn't even been able to write a note because she couldn't think what to put in it—and he was wrong, keeping her away from Maybelle, because he would never find anyone who would be more caring.

She said, 'I've done the work she left for me.' And she recounted in matter-of-fact tones what she had accomplished today. She knew what he thought about her but she was both competent and intelligent and she would have liked to scream that at him. As an afterthought she went on, 'She needs taking care of; well, you seem to realise that, but I wish you'd stop her carting jewellery around in her purse. I'm no expert, but she said the rings were real and they must be worth thousands.'

This was news to him. 'I didn't know that,' he said.

'So you don't know everything.'

'Obviously not,' he said wryly. 'You haven't mentioned this to anyone else?'

'Of course I haven't,' she snapped. 'So if she does get her bag snatched don't think I set it up.'

This time his words were lost as somebody shouted, 'Robin.'

She had clean forgotten Dominic, and it was Marc who called back, 'In here.' She could feel a bubble of hysteria building up in her lungs, and when Dominic arrived in the doorway she was holding down a nervous giggle because this was a familiar scene—Dominic looking hot and bothered, Marc cool and contained.

'You're back early,' Dominic blustered.

'I am,' said Marc.

Then Dominic saw Robin and croaked, 'What have you done to your hair?'

'I cut it,' she said. 'What do you think happened, it shrank in the rain?' If she did start shrieking with hysterical laughter it would be Marc who would slap her face and tell her to pull herself together.

'You shouldn't have done that,' said Dominic. 'It was beautiful hair. But you're still one of the most gorgeous girls I've ever seen. Well, I'm here. Are you coming?'

He was psyching himself up to defy Marc, and it was pathetic because he had never seemed less mature. He was boyish in every way, compared with Marc's potent and powerful masculinity.

'Going where?' asked Marc.

'Paris,' said Dominic. 'For the weekend.' His voice quavered as he tried to meet Marc's glare.

Without turning his head Marc looked piercingly at Robin, asking her, 'Is that why your case is packed?'

'Where is your case?' Dominic was jittering as if he wanted to grab her hand and run with her from the room.

If she went with him now—not to Paris, of course— but if she left the house with Dominic she would have her little triumph and small revenge on Marc. Briefly she might seem like the winner.

'You can't stop us,' Dominic shrilled.

Marc didn't give Dominic a second glance; his eyes were fixed on Robin. 'Robin,' he said, 'don't go.'

It wasn't an order, it was a plea, and of course she couldn't even pretend to be leaving with Dominic. He was making a nuisance of himself but it would be unkind to let him imagine she might, so she said gently, 'Dominic, this was never on; I'm leaving here but I'm not going with you. I'm packed to go back to my family.'

'You're taking the money,' Dominic shouted. 'He's bought you off.' And she felt less bothered about hurting his vanity when he was behaving like a brat.

'I'll see you out,' said Marc, and Dominic went on protesting as Marc gripped his arm and marched him away. Robin remembered Jack, the biker, getting thrown out bodily by Marc, and wondered if Dominic's feet were touching the floor, going down the hall to the front door.

It was only a few minutes before Marc was back, and she was ready for him, getting in what she was going to say quickly. 'And don't you ask me how much, because nobody needs to offer me anything for keeping away from Dominic.'

'Why didn't you say so before?' He was glaring at her again.

'I do apologise—' she made that heavily sarcastic '—but, as you've guessed, I'm not sugar-sweet under the skin, and I thought you deserved a bit of aggravation.'

'A bit of aggravation,' he roared, as if what she was saying was beyond belief. 'You thought that's what it was? Well, you were never more wrong in your life. Let's walk.'

'Walk where?' In the garden, it seemed. When he opened the door she said, 'It's raining.'

'Good,' he said. 'Clear the air.'

She went at his heels through what was turning into a downpour. There was nothing else she could do, and she had to hear what was coming next. He said nothing until they reached the seat under the horse-chestnut tree, then, again with a hand under her elbow, he seated her on it but stayed standing himself.

'You're not interested in Dominic?'

'No.'

'You never were?'

'*No.*'

'Then why the hell didn't you say so?' He didn't raise his voice that much, but it seemed to her as if he were shouting, looming over her, blocking out the trees and the sky. 'When I was offering cash why didn't you get angry? You usually go off like a firecracker. Why didn't you blow your top instead of saying you'd think about it? Going off to meet him, letting him think he was taking you to Paris. Why *did* you meet him?'

She told him why, zany though it sounded. 'Because you ordered me not to and I was taking no orders from you.'

'Good grief,' he exploded. 'If I'd told you not to jump in the river would you have jumped?'

'Yesterday,' she said, 'very likely.'

'What in the name of all that's holy are you playing at?'

'I'm not playing at anything.' Well, she had been, but only because he was cheating her. She sat rigid, glaring back. 'They said you were stringing me along because Lucy was scared Dominic had a crush on me. She asked you to break it up, didn't she?'

'Lucy? Yes.'

'Leila told me you were putting a stop to it. And Dominic said so. So did you.'

'I was. Not so much for Lucy, I can tell you, but because it was *aggravating* me, as you put it, out of my mind. Starting with watching you flirting with Dominic when you were dancing and finishing with your going off with him so that I didn't know what I was going to find when I followed you out there.'

His face was gaunt now and his voice was desperate and pleading. 'Jealousy is a new experience for me. I don't know how to handle it.'

Jealousy, she thought; I knew it when Leila was whispering to you, and it hurts terribly. And suddenly her face was pressed against him, muffling her voice as she whispered, 'Hold me. That's how you handle it.'

His arms could not have been tighter around her. Marc Hammond, needing her as badly as she needed him. They clung together wordlessly, as if they would hold each other as long as they lived, and it seemed incredible that they had not always known how right it would be.

Then she asked, 'When? For you?'

'In the hospital that first night,' he said. 'When your uncle was unconscious and you were telling him, "I love you so very much," I thought that if you ever said that to me it would bring me back from the dead. I've heard it from women before but I never needed to hear it. Until you said it it had only been words.'

'You never said it,' she said, and he smiled.

'I thought, Patience. Go slowly. Don't rush the girl. Get to know each other so that she'll understand this is the real thing.' She was smiling too. 'Because it is,' he said. 'You know that.'

'Yes, I know it.'

'So tell me. Please.'

'I love you so very much,' she said. It was the truth and always would be, and she had thought before that he had the nicest smile of anyone she knew, but this smile was for her alone and it was sending her wild.

'I want all of you,' he said. 'I want you body and

soul and spirit.' He wanted the essence of her that no other man could reach and she was looking at a man no one but she could see. 'I love you,' he said.

'Don't tell me,' she whispered. 'Show me.'

'I could do both.'

As the yearning rose in her, sending her breathless, she threw her head back, spluttering as the rain hit the back of her throat. It was streaming through the leaves, too heavily for the leaves to shelter them, making her choke and cough, and Marc said, 'Do we make a dash for it? I can't promise to keep my hands off you until we reach the house. Will you chance being ravished on the lawn?'

She hadn't noticed they were getting soaked till now. 'I'll risk it if you will,' she said, and they ran hand in hand out of the copse and across the grass, coming into the house laughing.

Rain spangled her lashes and lay like a shining helmet on his thatch of dark hair. He drew her within his arms, but held her a few inches away so that he could look at her from head to foot, and she whispered, 'What are you seeing?'

'You,' he said. 'And I'm wondering how I made it through the rain.'

Then they were into the kitchen, where they were dripping onto the tiled floor, and she gurgled, 'The grass would have been softer.'

'I'll make love with you in the kitchen some time,' he said. 'On the stairs, under the stars—anywhere. But this time I'd prefer it to be more traditional. Do you mind?'

Suddenly she was a bride—filled with wonder and a little shyness as he led her up the stairs into a room she hadn't seen before. She would have let her hair fall over her face if she hadn't hacked it all off. She had never needed a veil before, but her eyes were downcast as she felt his fingers brushing her skin, stripping her clothing away.

She hardly needed to help at all. His touch was so deft and so tender and everything fell away easily. But she watched, through lowered lashes at first, as he stripped, and then she seemed to know every bone and sinew in the hard-muscled body as if they had been lovers for years and had always been besotted with each other. And he was so beautiful that he could dazzle her in the dark.

He carried her to the bed, kissed her gently at first, so that little warm waves lapped her as if she were floating in a summer sea. Her lips were full, soft, parted, and her eyes were emerald-bright as she dug her fingers into his shoulders, locking herself to him and wondering how she could ever have thought she was frigid when, with this man, her body was giving such exquisite pleasure. For her and for him.

If he was leading it didn't matter, because she reacted instinctively, every move bringing a keener joy. Everything he did, everywhere she touched made her blood sing and her senses throb with a wild, sensual beat. She was high on happiness, drunk with delight, until the piercing spasms of fusion made her cry out, holding him tighter as he pulled her closer.

Her climax was out of orbit, soaring in a white-hot flame until she had no strength left, but floating her down again to where she lay, still on a cloud but spent, sleeping, maybe.

Maybe not. Eyes still closed, she reached out a hand and there was no one beside her. That raised her head, but Marc came out of the bathroom and smiled at her. 'Join me in a shower?' he said.

'I already have.' Rain was gleaming on the window-panes and she was suddenly and surprisingly refreshed. 'But a warm one would be nice.'

She knew her breasts were firm and high, her waist slim, and nakedness between them seemed natural. His muscles rippled, smooth as bronze, and she thought, You are superb, and teased, 'You shouldn't wear clothes, except perhaps a loin cloth. You look wonderful like this.'

He grinned. 'That's my line. Why does anyone as lovely as you have to wear anything?'

'Because,' she said gaily, 'if we strolled down the high street we might frighten the horses.'

'And,' he said, 'I don't think I could stand the pace.'

'The pace?'

'Killing all the men who looked at you.'

'Maybelle wouldn't like that.'

'Maybelle,' he said, 'is in for a pleasant surprise.'

'You think so?'

'I'm sure of it.'

This bathroom was bigger than hers, a man's bathroom as his had been a man's bedroom. The shower was on and she stepped under with him. Water cascaded over them, making her skin tingle as his thumbs massaged her shoulderblades and down her spine, and he was so close that he seemed to be part of her, drawing her into him as she was drawing him deep inside her.

Water filled her eyes and her ears until she was lifted high on a wave, arms and legs wrapped around him, head burrowed onto his chest. It was joyous and hilarious and she screamed with delight—'Yes, yes, *yes*!'—laughing as at last the water was turned off.

He wrapped her in a huge towel and carried her back to the big bed and laid her down on it. Then he lay beside her, still glistening wet himself, arms behind his head. 'Now, that,' he said, 'was far and away the best shower I ever had.'

She draped her towel around them both and curled against him, feathering her lips in the damp hair of his chest, listening to his heart in his ribcage. 'It was lovely,' she said. 'How long has this been going on? Why did I always see you around town as if I was looking for you?'

'Because we were looking for each other,' he said. 'When I saw you I always thought, There she is again; who is she with and what is she up to now? I should have caught up with you and said, This may come as a shock to you, Miss Johnson, but would you consider becoming as obsessed with me as I seem to be with you?'

She said gravely, eyes dancing, 'It would have been a shock.'

'To me too.'

But perhaps it would not have been that crazy. She had certainly been obsessed by him, although she hadn't known he was noticing her. 'It was probably the hair,' she said. 'Why you noticed me. Making me look like a tramp.'

'Sorry about that,' he said ruefully. 'I told you I couldn't handle jealousy. When I thought you might be having an affair with Dominic I didn't know what I was saying.'

'It didn't make me look like a tramp?' She raised her face now, her chin on his chest, looking up at him.

She could just see where a beard would grow along his jawline.

'No.' He denied it, then grinned. 'Well, if it did it was a very classy tramp.'

'I could have lived with that. I'm beginning to feel sorry I cut it.' And created a scene, leaving the hair strewn all over the drawing-room carpet. 'Were you going to laugh at me? Did you think it was funny when I cut it?'

She was smiling wryly but he didn't smile back. He said, 'God, *no*, it nearly broke me up. What I felt was tenderness, I suppose. I wanted to take care of you and stop you ever hurting yourself. I picked up the hair and put it away before I sent Elsie up to you.'

That could have moved her to tears if she hadn't blinked fast. She sniffed slightly and said, 'My hairdresser friend said it would have made a good hair-piece.'

'Uh-uh. And if you grow it again don't do that again.'

'That was temper. I went a bit ballistic. I don't do that often.' She let a few moments pass then admitted, 'Only with you.'

'Nor do I,' he said promptly. 'Only with you. Shall we take turns—' an eyebrow rose '—or only go crazy together, when we're on our own?'

She laughed. 'That sounds more fun.'

He could send her spinning out of control at a touch, and, with a little practice, she felt she might do the same for him. She was running a fingertip along his jawline when he asked, 'Do you want to go to Paris?'

'I don't know. I've never thought about it.'

'I'll take you when you do,' he said. 'I'll fly you where you want to go.'

She sat up, propping herself on an elbow, recalling, 'Maybelle said you had a pilot's licence.'

'And a plane.'

'Will you teach me to fly?'

'If that's what you want I will.'

She would love it, she thought. She said, 'I'd like that.' But Paris brought Dominic to mind, so she grimaced. 'Oh, dear!'

'Why "Oh, dear"?'

'I'm sorry about Dominic. I should have told him earlier not to be an idiot.'

'Don't worry about Dom,' Marc said cheerfully. 'There'll be no more trouble from him.'

And that made her wonder, 'What *did* you say to him?'

'You'll get more respect and less drooling from now on.' He had been still lying with his arms behind his head, now he sat up. 'I told him you were marrying me. Not this month. Perhaps not next. But soon. I wasn't sure you knew it at the time but I did.' Her breath caught and he said, 'You are marrying me, aren't you?' and tilted her chin so that he was looking into her eyes, and in his eyes she saw such love and commitment that it seemed as if their vows had already been taken.

She said, 'Oh, yes,' softly on a breath, happiness warming her like wine.

When he brushed back the damp tendrils from her forehead his fingers trembled although his voice was light. 'Another reason for making it legal. The hairpiece could be an heirloom for our daughter.'

He was stroking her hair and sending lovely little tremors rippling to her nerve-ends. 'I have a feeling this is going to run in the family,' he said.

He meant the colour, and she said, 'Oh, dear,' again, but smiling this time.

She was not clairvoyant but she had never been so sure of her future, and that the children would come—everything would come—because she and Marc were meant for each other. She said, almost drowsily, 'Maybelle thought you and me together would be fireworks,' and he laughed and kissed her eyelids.

'There will be,' he said. 'I promise.'

There surely would. There would be excitement and adventure and sparks flying upwards, because together they could set the world on fire. And always the haven of his arms and the wonder of their love. 'I love you so,' she whispered.

'You had better, my dear one,' he said, 'because you are my reason for living.'

He was caressing her slowly and sensuously and they matched each other so well, the softness of her with the hardness of him. When she stirred ever so slightly she could fit into the rise and fall of his long, strong body. She could feel his heart beat with her heart, their breaths mingling.

'Oh, yes,' she whispered, 'this is the reason,' and melted into him.

MILLS & BOON®

Next Month's Romances

♡

Each month you can choose from a wide variety of romance novels from Mills & Boon. Below are the new titles to look out for next month from the Presents and Enchanted series.

Presents™

WICKED CAPRICE	Anne Mather
A LESSON IN SEDUCTION	Susan Napier
MADDIE'S LOVE-CHILD	Miranda Lee
A HUSBAND'S REVENGE	Lee Wilkinson
MARRIAGE-SHY	Karen van der Zee
HERS FOR A NIGHT	Kate Walker
A WIFE OF CONVENIENCE	Kim Lawrence
THE PLAYBOY	Catherine O'Connor

Enchanted™

LIVING NEXT DOOR TO ALEX	Catherine George
ENDING IN MARRIAGE	Debbie Macomber
SOPHIE'S SECRET	Anne Weale
VALENTINE, TEXAS	Kate Denton
THE BRIDE, THE BABY AND THE BEST MAN	
	Liz Fielding
A CONVENIENT BRIDE	Angela Wells
TO LASSO A LADY	Renee Roszel
TO LOVE THEM ALL	Eva Rutland

Available from WH Smith, John Menzies, Volume One, Forbuoys, Martins, Woolworths, Tesco, Asda, Safeway and other paperback stockists.

The town of Hard Luck is a town that needs women...

The 150 inhabitants are mostly male but the three O'Halloran brothers have a plan to change all that!

An exciting new mini-series in the Enchanted line, written by one of our most popular authors,
Debbie Macomber.

"Debbie Macomber's Midnight Sons is a delightful romantic saga. Each book is a powerful, engaging story in its own. Unforgettable!"

—Linda Lael Miller

Look out for:
Falling for Him in January 1997
Ending in Marriage in February 1997

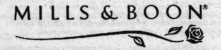

FREE!

FOUR FREE
specially selected
Enchanted™ novels
PLUS a Mystery Gift
when you return this card...

Return this coupon and we'll send you 4 Mills & Boon® Enchanted™ novels and a mystery gift absolutely FREE! We'll even pay the postage and packing for you.

We're making you this offer to introduce you to the benefits of the Reader Service™– FREE home delivery of brand-new Mills & Boon Enchanted novels, at least a month before they are available in the shops, FREE gifts and a monthly Newsletter packed with information.

Accepting these FREE books and gift places you under no obligation to buy, you may cancel at any time, even after receiving just your free shipment. Simply complete the coupon below and send it to:

MILLS & BOON READER SERVICE, FREEPOST, CROYDON, SURREY, CR9 3WZ.

No stamp needed

Yes, please send me 4 free Enchanted novels and a mystery gift. I understand that unless you hear from me, I will receive 6 superb new titles every month for just £2.10* each, postage and packing free. I am under no obligation to purchase any books and I may cancel or suspend my subscription at any time, but the free books and gift will be mine to keep in any case. (I am over 18 years of age)

N7XE

Ms/Mrs/Miss/Mr ——————————————————————

Address ——————————————————————

——————————————————————

——————————————————————

———————— Postcode ————————

Offer closes 31st July 1997. We reserve the right to refuse an application. *Prices and terms subject to change without notice. Offer only valid in UK and Ireland and is not available to current subscribers to this series. Readers in Ireland please write to: P.O. Box 4546, Dublin 24. Overseas readers please write for details.

You may be mailed with offers from other reputable companies as a result of this application. Please tick box if you would prefer not to receive such offers. ☐